Twice the Crime This Time

Maggie Pill

Publisher: Gwendolyn Press

This is a work of fiction. Names, characters, places, and incidents are products of the author's imagination or are used fictitiously and are not to be construed as real. Any resemblance to actual events, locales, organizations, or persons, living or dead, is entirely coincidental. All trademarks, service marks, registered trademarks, and registered service marks are the property of their respective owners and are used herein for identification purposes only.

Print Book ISBN: 9781393840015

Printed in the U.S.A.

Chapter One

Karen (Al & Karen from Pittsburgh) Jan. 21, 2020, 8:00 a.m.

For weeks now, my husband and I have been sniping at each other about windows. Our disagreement isn't about drapes versus curtains or blinds versus shades. It centers on whether the window coverings we already own should be open or closed. If Al had his way, every window would be blocked like Britain during the blackout. I wouldn't mind if we had no curtains at all. I mean, who cares if someone looks in our windows? All they'd see is a couple of seventy-plus fuddy-duddies doing nothing remotely interesting.

For the most part, I'm happy during our winters at B-Bird (official name: Beautiful Bird Over-55 RV Park), but the shut-in feeling of a trailer gets to me. Tiny rooms. Miniature closets. Sidling alongside the bed to reach those closets. It helps my mood to have the blinds up and the curtains open. Once we're dressed each morning, which is always early, I like to go around and let the light in.

Al objects. As I maneuver around his oxygen machine to reach pull-cords and turn tilt wands, he mutters things like, "People don't need to know what we're doing."

"What are we doing that's so secret?" I finally asked one day. "And why do we care if they know?"

He sniffed before replying, "Someone might see you in your underwear."

That made me chuckle. "Then someone will get exactly what he deserves: an eyeful of a dumpy seventy-two-year-old in granny panties and a full-figure bra."

Al's brow formed furrows that betray stubbornness. "It ain't right."

"No, it isn't right, because your fictional 'somebody' shouldn't be peeking in windows." I finished the task, and the argument, with, "I don't parade around in my underwear, so it won't happen anyway."

After several slightly adversarial conversations, Al started closing the living room curtains as soon as I went to the kitchen to start dinner. The first time, I watched as he lumbered from window to window shutting the place up like Fort Knox. When I came out to set his ration of pills beside his plate I asked, "Nobody's allowed to know we eat?"

His reply came in a tone that said further argument was pointless. "I like privacy."

The low-level, long-running discussion followed the path we've taken for decades. There's no outright fighting, but we each make comments over time to underscore the "rightness" of our opinions. I started mentioning that spending so much time in the dark made me feel like a mole. Al hinted at the possibility that I secretly enjoyed treating the neighbors to a peep show.

Dumb, but after fifty years of marriage, that's how we roll.

On a Tuesday afternoon in January, Al stumped into the house, his cane beating a faster tattoo than usual, and dropped a zinger. "We got a Peeping Tom in the park." There was a strong hint of "I tried to warn you" in his tone, which I ignored for the sake of household peace. A strong wind could blow my husband over these days, so I don't take after him with a frying pan, even when I should.

"Who told you that?" I was pretty sure I knew the answer. Hank Edmonds, Al's friend and the park's leading gossip, rides around on his bike like a town crier of old, picking up bits of information at one spot and passing them on at the next. Though Hank's not a bad guy, I often remind Al not to take everything he says as gospel. To enhance the drama of a presentation, Hank flavors facts with embellishments from his imagination.

"Hank heard it from Del," Al said. "At least three people have seen a stranger peeking in windows."

Since we'd had a murder at B-Bird only a month earlier, those sightings sounded more sinister than they would have before. "Did anybody ask the guy what he was doing in the park?"

"I don't think so. Clarence from Pelican Street called the office to let George know, but it was after five, so he was gone for the day."

"The sign at the entrance is clear about residents and guests only after six," I said. "Clarence should have called the police and reported the trespasser."

"Maybe he should have," Al said patiently. "I'm telling you what did happen, that's all."

"I hope people don't blow this all out of proportion." I was stirring chocolate to melt it for ice cream sauce, and I turned the heat down a little. "Remember when everyone said Riley Smith was dead?"

Al chuckled. "Yeah. First we heard he got killed in a car accident."

"Next, someone told us he was struck walking along the highway and was barely alive. A few hours later someone said he'd live but would be a paraplegic."

Al finished the story. "And then a few days later he came walking down our street with his arm in a sling, not dead, not at death's door, and by no means paralyzed."

B-Bird is like many closed communities in Florida, and I'd bet it's true in other places as well. Our residents are packed in close, so everything that happens draws notice and comment from the neighbors and anyone who might be passing by. In many cases we know each other but don't know each other, if you get what I mean. With three hundred sites, we see people every day but might not know their names, especially last names. As a result, people get confused about who is who. When someone tells a story, it's easy to picture the wrong person as the main character.

In addition to that, our residents are mostly retired and often idle. They're almost desperate for excitement, which is how information gets twisted and rumors get started. In the case of Riley Smith, I'd been interested enough to track down the source of the rumors. It turned out that the local news had reported that a resident of a completely different trailer park was killed in an accident on the highway. B-Bird resident Dennis Riley had mentioned in conversation that he'd almost been hit by a car as he crossed a busy street the day before. And Riley Smith had actually slipped in his own driveway and dislocated his shoulder. Only showing up in person was enough to prove that the rumors of his death were "greatly exaggerated." Mark Twain put it like that once when it happened to him. At B-Bird it happens all the time.

"As far as this Peeping Tom goes," I told Al, "we should wait and see what's true and what's imaginary."

"It wasn't Hank making stuff up. Other people have seen the guy and reported him to the office. George is trying to figure out what to do about him."

George, the park manager, is pretty level-headed, so I had to admit there was something to Hank's report. Trying not to sound grumpy, I said, "Maybe closing the curtains is good, but can we at least wait until it starts getting dark outside?"

"Fine with me."

Disagreements between Al and me are rare, and as soon as one of us admits he might be wrong, the other turns magnanimous. The rest of Al's comment revealed the real reason for his yen for privacy. "I don't like people gawking in when I take my breathing treatments. You have to watch me suck in Albuterol like a dope fiend, but you're stuck with me. I'd rather not have anybody else watching."

Chapter Two

Julie (Ron & Julie on Egret Street) Tuesday, 9:00 a.m.

Ron's physical therapist says the progress with his new knee is better than average, but he isn't ready to go back to golfing yet. When he looked sad, the guy suggested he might ride along in the cart with his buddies. I have to say it: I felt like a kid let out of school. Four times a week now, a car pulls up outside, picks my husband up, and takes him away for a few hours. The others play their round, Ron gets to be with them, and for a blessed few hours, I have the trailer all to myself.

B-Bird Park, in Vienna Hills, on the gulf side of Florida, is a great place to spend the winter, at least it was until Ron had surgery and I had him underfoot every day for weeks. Trailers are small spaces at the best of times, but when one of you is limited in activity level and pouty because he's bored, things can get tense. When Ron couldn't golf, couldn't shop, couldn't carry out his usual home repairs, he turned his attention to "helping" me with the housework. Since his help usually consists of doing part of a chore, it makes me crazy. He might take out the trash by emptying two of the waste baskets and leaving the other two half-full. Or he'll wash some of the dishes, and leave the rest in the sink. There's no logic to what he washes and what he leaves behind. It's apparently based on the whim of the moment.

The worst part has been Ron's campaign to rearrange the trailer, making it more "efficient." Last week I couldn't find a single pair of scissors anywhere…until I located all four pairs hanging on hooks on the back of the pantry door. I'm supposed to keep the spices in alphabetical order now, though Ron has no idea how often I need rosemary or mace.

When I retired from the library, I swore I'd never have anything to do with the Dewey Decimal System again. One day while I was out, my husband brought Dewey back, at least according to his concept of book cataloguing. In a floor-to-ceiling unit in the living room, I had shelved our books in a balanced, eye-pleasing way, with colorful figurines and knick-knacks spaced among them for interest. Now the figurines are all crowded on the middle shelf and the books are grouped by genre: history on the top shelf, historical novels next, and then detective stories. A dozen miscellaneous books, the kind Ron picks up at flea markets and will never, ever read, fill the bottom shelf. The subjects range from how to grow vegetables inside to why the Russians are better adapted to the cold than we are.

What I'm saying is that the weeks since Ron's surgery have been a trial. I try not to be grumpy about his attempts to be helpful, and he seems sad that I'm not more enthusiastic about them. Now that he's able to get out of the trailer, I'm hopeful he'll lose interest in where things are kept and go back to simply asking me to fetch them for him.

On Tuesday morning, Ron was out with the golfers and I was in the middle of folding laundry when someone knocked at the door. Expecting it to be Karen or Alice, I called, "Come on in," and finished the socks I'd been pairing. When I went out to the lanai, I found the police detective who'd investigated a murder in the park a few weeks before Christmas. "Oh." I pressed a hand to my chest in a gesture that was probably overly dramatic. "Detective O'Connor, right? I hope there hasn't been a—"

He put up a hand. "As far as I know, everyone here is alive and well."

I could have argued the "well" part. B-Bird is, after all, full of old people, which means many residents aren't in the best of health.

"What can I do for you?"

"Is your husband at home?"

"He's out, which thrills me more than I can say." I'd forgotten that O'Connor doesn't have much of a sense of humor. He obviously didn't know how to take my comment, so I added, "It's good for Ron to get out in the fresh air."

"Oh. Right." He frowned, and I concluded he had something he wanted to talk with both of us about. He was trying to decide if he should tell me now or come back when Ron was home.

"Can you sit for a minute? I made oatmeal cookies."

"Oatmeal?" O'Connor's formal manner disappeared. Though probably in his mid-thirties, he reminded me of the serious little boys who used to come into the library, get right up close to my desk, and ask where I kept the books on dinosaurs. Apparently cookies brought out the boy inside the man. "They're my favorite."

"Have a seat. Would you like a glass of iced tea?"

"That would be great."

As I plated some still-warm cookies I said, "Karen from Pittsburgh said she saw you at the park office yesterday."

"Karen who?"

I turned to the fridge to get the iced tea out. "Around here people seldom use last names. It's more about how we know each other."

"Oh."

He seemed confused, so I explained. "We have several Karens, so my friend is called Karen from Pittsburgh to distinguish her from Blond Karen or Karen on Gull Street. Alice across the street is stuck with being 'Tommy's new wife,' because most people still remember his first wife, Ella."

"What do they call you?"

"Most of the time I'm 'Ron's wife Julie.'" I gave him a wry smile. "Lately it's been 'Julie that almost got murdered.' That kind of thing sticks with you."

"You were lucky."

"I was." I set tea for each of our places at the table and the plate of cookies slightly toward O'Connor. "Will there be a trial?"

It turned out the detective liked his iced tea sweet and his oatmeal cookies in batches. The four I'd served up were gone before he finished updating me on the case that had led to our initial meeting. Rising, I set a few more cookies on the plate, recalling the days when I'd fed my son and his pals several times a week. Boys appreciate food like nobody else, and feeding them always makes me feel I've done something worthwhile.

After updating me as to whether I'd have to testify in court (It wasn't likely), O'Connor turned to the reason for his visit. "Yesterday I talked with the park secretary, Miss Doyle, about what I'm going to propose to you and Mr. Rogers. I asked her to keep it confidential, and she will. I'm going to ask you not to repeat anything I tell you as well." He paused. "Except to your husband, of course. He'll have to be in on it if you agree to help us."

"Help who? The police?"

"Yes. You two were pretty sharp during the events of last month. When another matter came up, I told my boss you might be able to find out things we need to know."

I felt a shiver go down my back, half excitement, half fear. I'd almost died for sticking my nose into the recent murder investigation, so that wasn't a pleasant memory. Still, O'Conner said Ron and I had been "sharp." Since age often brings loss of mental acuity, it was nice to hear we still have ours. "I'd need more information, Detective."

He nodded. "It's a cold case, which is why my captain is okay with involving the two of you. We don't think the guy we're looking for is dangerous. He's around eighty years old now, but back in the sixties, he killed two people."

"The sixties? What makes it of interest now?"

"A woman who dated the suspect back when the murders happened died recently. In her unopened mail was a letter from an old coworker, claiming her old boyfriend lives here at B-Bird Park."

"Oh." What else was there to say to that?

"Knowing her mother had once dated a man who turned out to be a killer, the woman's daughter sent the letter to the police." O'Connor paused. "Not sure why a mother would tell her daughter about something like that."

"I'd say it was meant as a warning to be careful who you associate with. Moms do that."

O'Connor nodded, accepting my expertise on parenting, and took another cookie. Between bites, he told the story. "This woman, Kelly Ames, worked at a restaurant in Nashville, Tennessee, in 1967. That spring she took up with a trucker, Greg Miles, who used to stop in when he rolled through town. They got close, and soon he was showing up almost every weekend. After a few months, Miles told Kelly he planned to quit over-the-road trucking and get a job nearby so they could get married." He finished his cookie and took a sip of tea. "One night she came home from work and found him waiting near her bus stop. He had blood on his shirt, but it wasn't his and he apparently wasn't aware of it. Miles said he had to leave for a while, but he'd send for Kelly when he could. She hardly had time to get what he was telling her before he was gone. She went on to her apartment building, where she learned that the young couple in the apartment below hers had been stabbed to death."

"How did she react to them suspecting her boyfriend of the crime?"

"She was shocked, but the blood on his shirt and his wild behavior convinced her. She told the police everything she could about Greg Miles." He sipped at his tea. "What she knew wasn't much help, because almost everything he'd told her turned out to be false. He was a trucker, but he wasn't from Kansas, he wasn't related to Conway Twitty, and his name wasn't Greg Miles." He paused to let that sink in. "DNA wasn't a thing back then, of course, and they didn't find any unexpected fingerprints at the scene. Still, two witnesses told a pretty damning story. A woman saw Miles hanging around outside the building before the murders happened. The landlord saw him come out of the couples' apartment at a dead run. He went inside and found the bodies."

"The girlfriend—Kelly—had no idea how to find a guy she'd been seeing for months?"

O'Connor shook his head. "I gather communication was kind of in the Stone Age back then." He glanced at me as if to see whether I took offense at that, but he was right, so I only nodded. "Kelly Ames didn't have a phone in her apartment, and the landlord was fussy about letting the tenants use his. She said when Greg passed through Nashville, he'd simply show up at the restaurant, and they'd make plans from there." Shaking his head, he added, "She didn't even have a photo of him."

"That wasn't unusual before the advent of cell phones."

"Right." His expression hinted he had trouble imagining a world without at least a hundred pictures on a device in his pocket. "Anyway, the cops ended up with a pretty general description: medium height and weight, sandy hair, blue eyes. They had Ames work with a sketch artist, and they circulated the drawing all over Tennessee, but they never found the guy. He probably left the state that night."

"It doesn't sound like much to work with all these years later."

"Right. But in her letter, Kelly's old friend claimed Greg Miles is here at B-Bird Park."

"And you think it might be true?"

O'Connor shifted in his chair, which led me to conclude he had doubts. "Frankly, Ms. Rogers, we've got plenty of current crimes to deal with. I can't devote a lot of time to a fifty-year-old murder case."

"But you need to check it out as a courtesy to the Nashville police."

"Exactly." Taking yet another cookie, he gave me a sheepish grin. "I won't have to buy any lunch today." Holding the treat at the ready, he made his proposal. "We can't interview every man over seventy in the park, and even if we did, the guy could say he was someplace else that night. How would we know he's lying?"

I saw the problem. It's easy today to check which truckers drive which routes and who was in a certain area code on a particular night, but fifty years ago? That was a big, "No way, Good Buddy."

"I suggested to my captain that you and your husband might do some digging for us."

O'Connor chewed on his cookie while I chewed on his words.

"What kind of digging?"

Holding up his free hand as if to stop me from panicking, he assured, "There's no danger. All you'd do is ask around and try to find out if a man living here drove long-haul semis in Tennessee in 1967."

"Why would he admit that if he's a fugitive from the law?"

"He might not see any harm in mentioning in casual conversation." He shrugged. "It's all we can think of to do."

I was struck by the idea that Ron and I might know a double murderer. It didn't seem possible. "Park management does a thorough background check before they let people move in here."

"Which is fine as long as the person is honest. This guy isn't."

"You're talking about a lot of men, Detective. Several hundred."

"That's true, but there's no time limit. Go at it any way you like."

I nodded. "I'll speak to Ron and see what he says."

"We'll appreciate anything you can do." Taking the last cookie, O'Connor rose. "We hate to turn down a request from another department, even if it's a real long-shot."

I rose too and, feeling we'd become better acquainted, made a personal remark. "I understand you and our park secretary are seeing each other."

He looked away in a classic "I'd rather not discuss that" manner. "Marlene and I do stuff together sometimes. It's nothing serious." He put out a hand, and we shook. "Let me know what you decide."

Chapter Three

Wilma (Wilma and Earl from the Michigan "Thumb") Tuesday, 11:00 a.m.

I've been kind of blue lately, and it might be because for the first time in my life, I'm unhappy in my marriage. No, that's not true. I'm not unhappy. I'm just not as happy as I used to be.

Earl has always been a gentleman, which means he looks out for me. Over our years on the farm, he'd bring me little gifts, a handful of wild raspberries, a few fresh mushrooms to add to a casserole, and the occasional egg some hen hid in the grass instead of laying it in the perfectly good nests we provided.

But recently I've started to feel crowded, maybe even smothered, by his constant attention. It makes me scream inside my head, "I'm not a child, for Pete's sake." I don't say it out loud though. That would be mean.

I think it started when we retired and left our farm in Michigan. On a hundred acres, we each had jobs to do each day, and while Earl was in and out of the house fairly often, he was busy getting the fields ready, planting and fertilizing them, and harvesting and storing the crops. Even in the wintertime he was outside a lot, keeping the snow at bay, repairing and maintaining his tools and machinery, and seeing to the livestock. I had my own chores, more of them inside, but I also saw to the vegetable garden, took care of the chickens, cooked, baked, and canned, and prettied the place up with flowers: crocus, daffodils, lilacs, iris, gladiolus, sweet peas, lily-of-the-valley, peonies, marigolds, and asters. I love color, and I filled our yard with as much of it as possible.

During those years, we were together but separate. Now that we're retired, we're together all the time. In addition, Earl has a lot fewer chores, since our plot of land in Florida is measured in feet, not acres. His equipment is shed-sized, not barn-sized, and there are no animals to tend to at all. The result is that most of my husband's energy goes into taking care of me.

On the day of choir practice, for example, I'll find my things laid out: a sweater on cool days, a broad-brimmed hat on sunny days, or an umbrella on wet days. When I set dinner on the table and go back to the kitchen for something, he's liable to have fixed my plate by the time I get back. And heaven forbid I should drive the car. If I want to go to the craft store, Earl's right there to take me, though there isn't a single item in the whole place he's interested in. He says to take all the time I want, but I always feel rushed when he's outside waiting in the car. I'd rather go by myself, wander the aisles, and look at every single thing.

Since all the hoo-ha last month over a murder here at B-Bird, it's gotten worse. Earl hovers around me like a bee that won't fly off and play with its other bee friends. If I leave the trailer without him, he acts like a dozen more killers are hiding in the shadows, waiting to fill me full of holes.

While I'm not particularly brave, I'm not mentally deficient either. With a killer at large, I traveled only with a group. I also stuck one of Earl's screwdrivers in the waistband of my pants, to defend myself if I was attacked. I kept an eye out for strangers. And I made sure Earl knew where I'd be.

It wasn't enough. He'd say, "Do you really need to go out?" and if I said yes, he'd say, "I'll walk with you and wait until you're ready to come back home."

The knitting needle killer got caught, and the danger is over. Life should be back to normal, but Earl still frets, all day, every day, about my safety. His idea of protection is for me to be with him every time I step outside the trailer.

We're on a pretty slim budget, so we don't go out to dinner or to movies every week, the way some do. Mostly we take advantage of activities offered in the park. This year Earl joined a woodcarving group that's making keepsake boxes for women in local homeless shelters. They're pretty, and they have tiny locks so the ladies have a place to put their rings and stuff in case someone in the place isn't honest. When Earl said some of the wives stain and varnish the boxes once the guys finish making them, I agreed to go to a session and try it out.

I can't say I cared for it much. In the first place it's boring for an experienced crafter like me to do only part of a project, and not the most creative part at that. When I told Earl I wasn't thrilled with staining little boxes, he said, "But it's something we can do together."

"We aren't together, Earl," I said. "You're with the men at the machines, and I'm with the women, getting stain under my fingernails and a headache from the fumes." He gave me a funny look, like he was hurt, but he gave up on dragging me to woodworking.

That wasn't the end of it. Earl decided I should go along and watch when he plays shuffleboard and pickle ball. Feeling bratty about not helping at the wood shop, I agreed, but it's…How do they say it? Like watching paint dry. Earl says it's good for me to get outside, and I suppose that's true, but I would really rather stay home and work on my projects. It bugged me when he said, "I like you being close, so I know you're okay."

Earl's fussing, and the resentment I feel about it, are starting to worry me. If I love the man, shouldn't I want to spend time with him? I've been asking the Lord to help me be less selfish, but I also confessed to Him how bad I hate pickle-ball. Yesterday Earl mentioned they're talking about starting up a lawn bowling league. "You'll like it," he said. "You can be my cheerleader."

I had to bite my lip to keep quiet, and I wonder, does my getting irritated with Earl mean I don't love him anymore? If I don't, what's going to happen to us? I truly believe marriage is for life, but sometimes I imagine how it would be to make my own decisions about where to go and when to come home. Then I picture Earl's sweet face, and I remind myself how lucky I am to have him.

The only time I get to myself these days is when Earl goes golfing, He tried to get me interested in that too, but after one time on the links, he dropped the idea. We spent more time looking for lost golf balls than anything else, and both my arms were black and blue from all the times my club hit the ground instead of the ball. Knowing he'd love another chance each week to lower his handicap, I tweaked our skimpy budget and announced we could afford for him to golf on Thursdays too.

As always, Earl's first thought was for me. "You'll be left alone four mornings a week."

I wanted to say, *And that will be restful*. Instead I said, "If I get lonely, I can always ask Julie or Alice to come over for coffee."

Chapter Four

Earl (Earl & Wilma from Michigan's Thumb)
Tuesday, 11:00 a.m.

Wives should always be dead sure their husbands care about them. Wilma and me don't have a lot of what they call worldly goods, but we do okay. We had a farm in southeast Michigan, but when we were ready to retire, we turned it over to family instead of selling the land to some developer to build condos on. We live on Social Security plus what our nephew pays on the land contract each month. That means we don't have a fat retirement, but we're pretty good at cutting corners. Wilma was a recycler long before it was all the rage, and she comes up with clever ways to reuse things and save money. I'm okay with that, even if I get a blister from wearing socks that are darned. I forget sometimes and do things that irritate her, like throwing away the little skewer they give you at the grocery store when you taste-test a new product. Wilma uses them as stakes to support the seedlings she starts every spring. We don't have fields to take care of anymore, but you should see our back porch in Michigan. It's loaded with everything from tomatoes to coriander—whatever that is.

My wife is so clever it amazes me. She can make something out of nothing, and she always has exactly the right thing in one of her bags to make a gift prettier or to hide a stain or a hole in my shirt. Because she's creative, she isn't always practical, so I figure that's where I can help. Wilma never thinks ahead. If the sun is shining, she acts like it will shine all day long. If she has enough flour to make a cake today, she doesn't think about the pie she'll want to make next. I make it a point to be watchful and show her I still care, even after all these years.

We first came to B-Bird a few years ago in search of a second home that's warmer than our regular one. We picked this park at random, but we stayed because everybody here is real nice. I like that it's all older people, with no smart-aleck teenagers around to hassle us. A friend of ours has a nice condo in St. Pete, but he says that during Spring Break the kids are a real pain, making noise all night and breaking the bulbs in the street lamps.

After the murder in December, I realized we weren't as safe as I'd thought. Since then, I've been more careful about watching over Wilma. I don't want my girl to ever have to worry about the bad things that can happen. I can't buy Wilma fancy cars or whatever, but I was trained by the United States military, so I can look out for her. I understand that it was a long time ago, but a guy doesn't forget how to stand between the people he cares about and those that want to hurt them.

Not that I'm one of those paranoid types. B-Bird is a pretty safe place, and George has done what he could to beef up security since the murder happened. He sent us all a letter saying what's being done to keep everyone protected, and I think he'll do his best to see to it.

We've got some oddballs in the park. Matthew Nowicki, who lives on Hawk Street, is one of those conspiracy nuts, always telling how the U.S. government is controlled by aliens or some such nonsense. If you can ignore that, Matthew isn't a bad guy. He's always helping with events, and the ladies appreciate a man who's willing to let them order him around.

Then there's Del Hanna on Egret Street, who brings a new woman to Florida every year. I try not to judge others—that's God's job—but I doubt Del meets his "ladies" at church, if you know what I mean. Still, he's got his good side. Del sounds exactly like Pat Boone when he sings. Somebody talked him into joining the choir, and his voice adds a lot. It's probably good for him to hear the sermon every week too, but again, it's not my place to judge.

There's a woman on Crane Street, Olive Something, who talks to the birds. She doesn't do it the way a normal person might, "Nice bird," or, "You're a fine-looking fellow." She argues with them, apparently on topics such as tax evasion, and it can go on for twenty minutes at a time. When she goes back north this summer and her kids see how far gone she is, I figure Olive won't be coming back to B-Bird. In the meantime we all look out for her, checking to see she remembers to eat and whatever.

So we have some odd people here, but we also have lots of normal ones, and a nice, natural setting too. In modern Florida, nature is too often stuffed into corners circled by six-lane highways. For my whole life before this, I had a few hundred acres all to myself, so most places I go around here feel crowded. Still, the park is set off the highway, and the lake and the trees to make you forget you're in the middle of one of the most tourist-dense states in the union. It gets pretty quiet at night, and I like to go down to the shore late and listen to the critters. Some, like the squirrels and songbirds, are getting ready for a good night's sleep. Others, like the raccoons and coyotes, are sticking their noses out to see what they can find to eat. I often sit on a bench at the lake edge and listen to the world that isn't people. It helps a guy feel rested.

Last night I had kind of a shock. I got up to go and almost bumped into a guy when I stepped onto the road. It was too dark to see more than a black shape, but he made that "Ope!" sound people make when they're surprised. "Sorry," I said. "I didn't mean to scare you."

"It's okay," he muttered, and in a second he was gone. I didn't recognized the voice, but there are plenty of people in the park I've never met. Another man who enjoys the feeling of being alone for a while, I figured. At night it's easier to forget how crowded life is in a trailer park, even a nice one like ours.

Chapter Five

Alice (Tommy & Alice, the new wife) Tuesday, 1:00 p.m.

Though Tommy and I haven't been married that long, I've learned a few things about him. One is that he isn't a patient type. He is a good person, so for a friend who needs his help, Tommy will wait around all day. But when it's a task he sets for himself, the time he gives himself to do the job starts wide and then shrinks like a cheap T-shirt. Here's an example. A week ago, Tommy mentioned he was thinking about redoing the floor in our bedroom. The next day he stood in the doorway on and off all morning, making diagrams and calculations. "I'm going to do it," he told me at lunch. "Early in March, probably."

As I said, I've learned a few things, so I merely nodded.

Four days ago, he went out and bought the materials. "Sometimes you have to order flooring way ahead of time," he explained. "I want to make sure I've got what I need when I'm ready, maybe around the end of February." The next time he mentioned the project, the start date was mid-February.

Now it's tomorrow. The same thing happened with repainting our awnings, replacing the back steps, and painting the carport. I think it's cute, and he doesn't even realize he does it.

I was helping Tommy set up sawhorses in preparation for his project launch when the park manager stopped by. Tommy is head of the Resident Council, so he and George talk pretty often. "Got another project going?" he asked. Tommy stopped hauling and explained the plan in detail. George listened, nodded, and made noises of approval. (Men get such a thrill out of telling each other how hard they plan to work.) Since the sun was already becoming hot, I went inside, made a pitcher of lemonade (Tommy's favorite) and set it in the freezer to chill.

When I came back out, George was telling Tommy about the park's rumored Peeping Tom. "I keep getting reports," he was saying, "but the details don't match up. Some describe the guy as skinny; some say he's beefy. One person claims he hangs around empty trailers, but someone else saw him peering into the windows of a place that's occupied, though the owners were away." He gave an annoyed huff. "I asked our maintenance guy to take a walk after dark last night, but he saw nothing. He thinks it's all a bunch of talk. Somebody sees a stranger, starts a story, and it turns into a panic."

"Possible," Tommy agreed, "especially if the descriptions are all over the place."

"I can't ask Bill to patrol the park at night and still do his regular work in the daytime."

"Security isn't his job anyway." Tommy frowned. "Maybe we should ask residents to call the police if they see the guy."

"But the person could be someone's teenage grandson, handling his boredom by walking around looking at stuff." George sighed. "I hate to make a fuss after the negative publicity we had with a murder here."

"You couldn't have done anything to prevent that, George," Tommy said consolingly.

"Tell that to Ma—your fellow residents." I guessed George almost said "Matthew." While it isn't professional to gripe about one resident to another, Matthew Nowicki would test the patience of a saint. He's insufferably arrogant and completely unaware of it. Add to that the fact that Matthew has a conspiracy theory for everything, and you have a nightmare resident. He wasn't speaking to Tommy and me lately, due to some mischief on Tommy's part, but I figured that since the murder, George got a daily earful from Matthew on the topic of resident safety.

After George left, Tommy and I moved things around on the lanai so we could set the bedroom furniture out there. One of the trials of working on a trailer is there isn't enough room to swing a cat (which Tommy informed me is a phrase from the 1700s when the cat o' nine tails was used to punish sailors). There often isn't much room to swing a hammer either, so I put the small things in the bedroom into the built-in closets, and then Tommy and I moved the furniture, everything but the bed, onto the lanai.

When we stopped for a break Tommy said, "With any luck I'll get the flooring laid by tomorrow night."

"You've got friends who'd be glad to help."

"I know." Tommy tilted his head. "I like working alone. The guys give me a hard time about it, but I do."

"I doubt they're offended," I assured him. "Most want something to do, and they like you." With a grin I added, "Most of them."

That reminded him of something. "Matthew stopped me on the street the other day and asked if I could recommend an eye doctor."

"Matthew asked you for advice?"

Tommy grinned. "People like that can't stay mad at old enemies, because they're always making new ones. Matthew gave me his views on the health system in the U.S. It was pretty funny."

"Let me guess. Pharmaceutical companies have cures for every disease known to man, but they won't share them because they'd be out of a job."

"That's what he said."

"And your doctor is in cahoots with all the other doctors in town, cooking up schemes to make you spend your money on unnecessary tests and unwarranted procedures."

"He said that too. Matthew contends that optometrists actually give you cataracts so they can charge you when they remove them." Tommy grinned. "It's apparently in that little puff of air they shoot at you."

"No more puffs for me," I said with mock seriousness. "Did you provide the name of the one honest eye doctor left in all of Florida?"

"After some hesitation, I gave him Dr. Fanner's name." Tommy sighed. "I like the doc, and…"

I finished for him. "Recommending him to Matthew Nowicki is the equivalent of mailing a bomb to his office."

Chapter Six

Ron (Ron & Julie on Egret Street) Tuesday, 3:00 p.m.

While she made burgers for me to cook on the grill, Julie told me about O'Connor's visit. "Your friend the cop wants us to ferret out a guy who's been on the run for fifty years?" I asked.

"He isn't my friend," she responded. "He's a police detective who came to us for help."

"Snooping into the lives of the people we know."

A grimace revealed that part bothered her a little. "Do you want me to tell him no?"

"I didn't say that." To be honest, I was as pleased as she was to hear that O'Connor trusted us with the job. How many people over seventy get invited to conduct an undercover investigation for the cops? Though I didn't relish the idea of snooping among people we knew, this guy was a double murderer.

Doubt cropped up again. "It would be weird, sticking our noses in everybody's business."

"We helped them zero in on the Knitting Needle Killer. That wasn't weird."

"No, it was dangerous. You almost got murdered."

She nodded, accepting the truth of that, and her nails clicked briefly on the countertop. "What should I tell the detective?"

An idea came into my head. "Tell him a job like this is too big for two people."

"What does that mean?"

"It means that in order to canvass over three hundred residences, we should get some help." I ticked off my points on my fingers. "We'll get done faster, more people means a wider base of information, and best of all, you and I won't have to lie to the couples we're closest to."

Julie rested her chin on her hand. "I don't know if O'Connor will agree to that."

"If he wants us to do this, he will."

"They'd have be people who can keep a secret. And we'd need to be sure the men can't possibly be Greg Miles."

"Tommy was in Vietnam during the summer of 1967," I replied. "I've seen the pictures. Al Dobson never left the state of Pennsylvania until he retired from his factory job. And I'm pretty sure Earl was on a ship in the Pacific that whole year."

"And except for Tommy, they've all been married to the same woman forever," Julie added. "It isn't likely any of them was spending weekends with a woman named Kelly in Nashville." Biting her lip, Julie mulled it over. "I wish Cheri hadn't gone to that wedding back in Canada. She'd be good help."

"She probably wishes she hadn't gone too. I hear the weather up there is wild right now."

"I could pitch the idea of a group project and see what O'Connor thinks."

"It might be fun, all of us investigating a cold case together."

Julie chuckled. "Yeah. The Silver Sleuths of B-Bird RV Park."

Sensing she was nervous about asking O'Connor if we could change the plan around, I asked, "Do you want me to call him?"

"That would be great," she said. "If he doesn't go for it, you and I can discuss whether we want to proceed or opt out."

I called right away, since it was almost five. O'Connor answered, and after listening carefully to my arguments said, "That sounds workable, Mr. Rogers, as long as you vouch for the other three men." When I explained what I knew of their backgrounds he said, "Let me okay it with the boss. I'll get back to you in the morning."

"If it's a go, can we get more details on the case?"

"We can do that now if you like. I asked Nashville P.D. to scan the murder book and email it to me, and I was reading through it when you called." I heard his computer mouse click as he perused the pages. "The original detective assigned to the case, Dean Marshall, left lots of notes, which is good, since he died in '88. The girlfriend, Kelly Ames, thought she was in love with Miles, but when she realized he was a killer, she did a one-eighty and helped the cops all she could."

He went on, pausing briefly at times to read before filling me in. "Ames lived upstairs in an old house that was divided into four apartments. The landlord had a rule that single female tenants couldn't have men in their apartments. Since he lived on the ground floor, he got his way." O'Connor seemed struck by that. "Landlords could dictate their tenants' behavior like that back then?"

"You should have met Julie's house mother at college," I told him. "Try a goodnight kiss of more than ten seconds, and she'd be rapping on the window and pointing the Finger of Death at you."

"Huh. Anyway, the guy's rule meant the police couldn't get a sample of Miles' prints."

"What's the scenario? Why was this couple murdered?"

"Marshall's theory was that Miles broke in planning to rape the wife. He wasn't aware the husband had stayed home from work due to illness. The man was in the bedroom when he broke in, probably asleep. Hearing the struggle, he got up and came out. Miles had already stabbed the woman. She died instantly. The husband went after Miles, and they struggled. Miles stabbed the husband and ran, taking the knife with him. The report says the guy didn't live long, maybe a couple of minutes."

"Who called it in?"

"Anonymous."

"Huh. Who'd have known what was happening?"

There was another pause as O'Connor looked for a particular spot in the report. "The detective suspected it was the boyfriend of the tenant in the other upstairs apartment, Jill Carr. She's the one who wrote to Ames claiming Miles lives in your park. The women worked at the same place, so she knew him from times he came to the restaurant to see Kelly."

"And she recognized him all these years later?"

"Not by sight. It was his voice she recognized. Looks change, voices not so much."

"That's true," I agreed. "I've had the experience of hearing a voice from my past and knowing right away who it was."

"Me too." O'Connor went on. "Anyway, Marshall figured Jill's boyfriend was staying in her apartment, heard the commotion, and called the police. Later he didn't admit it was him because the nasty landlord would have kicked Carr out if he knew she had a man there."

"Could he have been the killer?"

"The guy was thoroughly checked out. No stains on his clothing, and Marshall says the stabbings would definitely have resulted in blood on the killer."

The image that brought to mind, a man and his wife bleeding out inside their own home, made the old crime real to me. This wasn't simply a puzzle for a bunch of old farts to work on. It was a search for the man who'd violently murdered two innocent people. I wanted to help the cops find him and lock him up for whatever remained of his miserable life.

Unaware of my thoughts, O'Connor went on. "By the time the police arrived, the landlord had called in the incident as well. He'd gone to a movie, and he was coming up the walk when a guy barreled out of the apartment, ran into him, almost knocking him down, and took off. Seeing the door to his tenants' apartment had been kicked in, the landlord went inside and found the bodies.

O'Connor paused to read. "Sounds like he was an emotional mess. Anyway, Kelly arrived a few minutes after the police did. She'd talked to Miles and was still shaken from his appearance and behavior. When she heard what had happened, she told them everything she could, including where he usually parked his truck. They found it in the parking lot of an empty building, wiped clean of prints. He did an excellent job on that, but he missed a muddy boot print he'd left on the accelerator pedal. It was a partial, but it matched the one left on the apartment door when he kicked it in."

"Julie said there was another eyewitness?"

"A woman waiting for the bus saw Miles arrive on foot around ten. She assumed he was waiting for a ride, but he didn't get on when the bus came."

"He was waiting for Kelly."

"Seems so. The description she gave matched what they had for Miles."

"Why would he break into the other apartment and attack a woman he didn't know?"

"Sex crimes are often spontaneous, the result of overwhelming emotions that normal people don't understand. He might have seen her through a window and got ideas. Or he might have heard from Kelly that the husband worked nights and took his chance."

"You'd think he'd have made sure the man was gone before trying anything, don't you think?"

"Like I said, it's often hard to explain sex crimes."

"Thanks for the information, Detective. Give us a call when your boss says we can start."

Chapter Seven

Al (Al & Karen from Pittsburgh) Tuesday, 4:00 p.m.

I was sitting on my porch, as usual, when Hank rolled up on his bike. Before his wheels had fully stopped he asked, "Did you hear about Rennie's scare?"

"No," I said. "Who's Rennie?"

"Long red ponytail."

"Oh, yeah. Married to Jack."

He nodded. "They rent down here every year, but this time they couldn't get the same place they had before. They took that trailer Jim rents out—Jim that fixes bikes."

"Tall guy, real white hair."

"Right. Anyway, Rennie's one of those clean freaks, so she won't let Jack unload a single thing from the car until she's scrubbed the place to her standards. So Jack is emptying the car and setting stuff on the porch, and he hears her screaming bloody murder. He goes running in there, and here's Rennie, jumping on the bed and stomping at something. 'Kill it!' she hollers. 'Jack, kill it!'

"Jack takes one look and starts laughing to beat the band. She was wiping out this long, high shelf over the head of the bed, and this hairy thing came flying out. Rennie thinks it's a scorpion or something, so she kicks at it with both feet and yells, 'Kill it, kill it!' Jack got her calmed down and showed her what it really was—a toupee the previous renter left up there."

"That's a good one, Hank." Between chuckles, he retold the story, as he often does. After we had a second good laugh, he pedaled off to tell it to someone else. I watched, a little enviously, as he accelerated down the street and then slacked off, leaning into the turn where Osprey Street meets the road that runs the perimeter of the park. I haven't been able to ride my bike for the last year or so, and I miss the feeling of speeding along smooth as silk.

We have lots of bicyclists at B-Bird, which might seem odd to some. In the world outside, you seldom see old fogeys on bikes, but here they pedal this way and that, some with baskets full of trash, some sporting those pricey fat tires, some on three wheels for stability, and in one case, an old-fashioned bicycle built for two. Cars are necessary for going outside the park, but here, bikes are useful for doing errands, for exercise, and for the sheer joy of feeling like a kid again.

Being unable to ride anymore makes me sad and a little mad, but life is what it is. I don't begrudge people like Hank the good health they manage to carry into their seventies and eighties, but I wish mine was a little better. Somewhere in my fourth decade, my whole body started disintegrating, my joints, my spine, my organs, everything. The doctors keep me going, but I gotta tell you, it isn't easy for them or for me.

My wife is the most wonderful woman in the world, though she'd slap me if she heard me bragging on her. For Karen, marriage is for better or worse, like they say in the vows. She never complains about getting the worst of 'for worse.' She does almost everything around the house these days, and while she sometimes takes the whole "bright, clean house" concept too far, she does a great job. It's amazing how good she's got at repairing stuff, and you might see her with a wrench or a screwdriver as often as with a broom or a bucket. On top of that, she sees to my appointments, medications, and therapy when I need it, which means making sure they're okay with my insurance and getting me to and from on the right days at the right times.

Karen does all this without ever hinting that I'm the burden I know I am. When I had carpel tunnel surgery and couldn't fasten and unfasten my own pants, she made jokes while she did it for me. When I fell and broke my elbow and the thing turned septic, she dealt with the mess with a no-nonsense approach and a bunch of smart remarks. And if I land the hospital with blood clots, pneumonia, or heart palpitations, she stands beside my bed, interpreting what the doctors say and making sure they know she's watching to see I get the best care.

I hate being so messed up that I can't sweep my own driveway or change the oil in my car. I try not to get down about it, but when Ron stopped by to say the police wanted our help with a sort of undercover investigation, I jumped at the chance.

I didn't tell Karen about it right away. For one thing, Ron said if the other two couples didn't agree, the plan might be scrapped. Also, I worried that Karen would say no. The search for a murderer was something she wouldn't approve of me being involved in, since stress tends to make some of my ailments worse. I could see her arguing that investigating a fifty-year-old crime wasn't worth me having a stroke or a heart attack. Still, if Ron got Earl and Tommy involved and their wives agreed to help, I thought I could convince Karen to join in.

Lighting up a cig, I batted questions around in my head. Who at B-Bird might be a killer? How would we go about finding him? Could we help the cops put him behind bars after all this time?

With something to look forward to, I continued to ignore the dizzy spells that had started over the last week or so, another sign my body doesn't function very well. I was careful about changing levels quickly, and I kept my cane close by for support. Otherwise, instead of dwelling on the negatives in my life, I pictured eight of us working together, planning, discussing, and winnowing relevant facts from an ocean of information. The best part was thinking that for once, I might be useful to the world again.

Chapter Eight

Karen (Al & Karen from Pittsburgh) Tuesday, 6:00 p.m.

Late Tuesday afternoon, Hank stopped by for his third visit of the day. I had a chicken roasting on the grill, so Al and I were on the porch, smoking and playing a few hands of gin rummy while our noses got teased by the mouth-watering smell of supper on the way.

Hank looked like he was about to burst, which meant his news was big. "George is planning to quit. They're interviewing for a new park manager."

Tossing away a queen, I frowned. "I thought he was happy here."

"Probably health issues." Al's health is seldom far from his mind, so he tends to think every decision a person makes stems from how he's feeling.

"Yeah." Hank's eyes widened. "Maybe he got a bad diagnosis."

"Now don't you two start making things up," I cautioned. "We don't know anything."

Removing his cap, Hank ran a hand over the sparse patch of white hair left on his head. "A guy sees things, and he puts 'em together. Most times he can figure out what's going on that way."

I didn't argue, though I could have tossed out a half-dozen times when Hank had seen "things," put them together, and reached a wrong conclusion. Al doesn't like it when I contradict Hank, but the man is far too likely to fill any gaps in information with speculation.

I try to make allowances, since he's good to his wife Janis, who's now in a long-term care facility. "How do you know George is quitting?"

"Well, I rode by the office around closing time—by the way, a brand new fifth wheel was pulling in on Cormorant, behind the office building. I'll stop on my way home and see if they need anything."

Hank has appointed himself unofficial greeter for newcomers to B-Bird. By sundown he'd know whether they came from New York or Illinois or Kansas and if they plan to stay a month, three months, or until Easter.

"When I passed," he was saying, "this sharp-looking guy in a suit was sitting in the lobby. I went inside to get a better look at him."

Taking a drag off my cigarette, I hid a little smile. It's amazing how causally Hank admits to being the nosiest person in the park.

"Right away I figured out what he was there for." Reaching in his shirt pocket, Hank got out a cigarette his own. "You can tell when someone's looking for a job, because they chat up the secretary like mad. This guy was definitely giving Marlene the soft soap."

"Maybe he wanted a date."

Hank waved that away, along with a puff of smoke from his own cig. "I can tell the difference between wanting a girlfriend and wanting a job." Though I doubted that, I waited for Hank to present the rest of his evidence. "I was kind of hanging around, pretending to read the notices on the board, and pretty soon Alice came in. She and Marlene talked, but I couldn't hear all of it." Hank's chin rose as he finished, "But I definitely heard Marlene tell Alice that George will be done by the end of the month."

I got up to check on the chicken as Al and Hank speculated on how the park might change with a new manager. Hank believed things would get "tightened up," and he had quite a few suggestions for how that should go. "They need to kick some of the people on Crane Street right out of here," he said firmly. "If they can't keep their places up, they need to get out."

Looking down the street, I saw Alice, carrying a rolled-up yoga mat. She was headed for the exercise room, but when I gestured, she turned into our drive.

"Chicken smells great," she said, leaning an elbow on the porch railing. "Tommy's making more of his famous chili." She kept her expression blank, but I heard criticism in her tone. Tommy was proud of his chili-making skills, but she'd shared her objections with me. "In the first place, he makes it about twice a month. In the second place, he doesn't know how to make a small batch, so we have to eat chili for six nights running."

Instead of commenting on chili I said, "Has Tommy mentioned anything new going on with park management?"

She gave me a questioning look. "No. I was just in the office, and things seemed normal. There was a salesman waiting to see George, but that's all.

In an innocent tone I asked, "A good looking guy in a suit?"

"Yes. I stopped to ask when the new water rates will go into effect, and George was showing the guy into his office." With a disapproving look she added, "Marlene says he wants to hold one of those Buy Your Gold events in our hall."

"Bet he won't get far with that idea."

"I hope not." I hid a smirk when Alice added, "Anyway, George told Marlene that he should be done figuring the new water rates by the end of the month."

"George will be done by the end of the month," I repeated.

Alice tilted her head a little. "Yes." She turned to Hank. "You were there. You must have heard her."

After a short silence Hank said, "I should get going."

"Yeah, buddy." Al's tone was a little too hearty. "See you later."

Chapter Nine

Tommy (Tommy & Alice, the new wife)
Wednesday, 7:00 a.m.

I'm the go-to guy for park residents planning renovation projects. Since most of us are transplants, and temporary ones at that, it's hard to keep track of Florida's rules for construction and renovation. As head of the Resident Council, I keep current on the statutes, so people often come to me for advice about what they're allowed to do under the law. Ron teases me sometimes for going on a bit too long on the subject, but it's important that people get facts, not somebody's sloppy opinion.

Wednesday morning, while I waited impatiently for quiet hours to be over, a guy named Ben came by to ask about the rules for repairing storm damage. A friend of his who lives farther north had lost part of his roof when the tail of a hurricane passed through his park, and he wondered how his buddy should proceed. As is often the case when a person stops to talk home repair, others show up, and soon I had a half-dozen men under my carport, some of them straddling bikes, others carrying their mugs of coffee.

I was pleased to be able to explain to Ben the relevant part of the Florida building code. "Once the extent of storm-related damage has been determined, you identify what building codes and requirements are in effect locally, since repair is governed at the local level. Generally, some version or derivative of the International Existing Building Code will be in effect, but they'll vary based on location. Your buddy might find current building codes on the local government's website, or he could call to confirm this information."

"Or he could fix it and keep quiet," someone commented. "Any time you can leave the government out of things, you're better off."

"I wouldn't go that route," I warned, "but people do what they do."

We were interrupted when Del, who lives a few lots down, joined us, looking rumpled and angry. The reason for his foul mood became clear when he said, "Shawna informed me at breakfast that her sisters want to come down and stay with us for spring break." He scrubbed at his hair with one hand. "What am I supposed to do with three extra adults and five kids in a frickin' trailer?"

Nobody had a good answer for that, though Harry offered the use of two blow-up mattresses he had in storage. Del didn't even consider it. "No. They aren't coming, and that's it."

Probably to bring an end to the topic, Ron brought up the peeper. "I keep hearing about this guy hanging around the park at night," he said. "Has anyone here seen him?"

"Shawna did," Del said. "She said he's way too young to live here, like twenty, and kinda skinny."

"That's not right." Ben is a loud talker, so the whole street probably heard his comment. "Big Frank saw him on Tuesday night. He says he's about thirty and built like a tank."

"Hank says he's got a big old beard," Harry put in, rubbing his chin to make the point.

"People come and go in this place," I said. "The guy could be a plumber's helper, an AC repair tech, a delivery man, a satellite TV installer, lots of things."

"Then why is he peeking in windows?"

"He might not be," I said calmly. "The simplest explanation is best. All the hookups for water and electrical are at the back of the trailers, so nobody should freak out when they see a man go past their window."

"What time of day did your lady see the guy?" Harry asked Del.

"After work hours," Del replied. "Maybe six-thirty."

Still trying to be logical I said, "Lots of times workmen are here late, trying to get the job done."

He clung to the dramatic version. "Shawna says he was definitely looking in Mark Carlson's window."

I gave up. "Listen, guys, I'm going inside. I've got work to do." They wandered off, Del still talking as Harry leaned his big body down to catch every word. Assuming the peeper was the topic, I shook my head. Rumors.

By the time Alice returned from grocery shopping that afternoon, I was putting the last section of flooring in place. "It looks beautiful, Tommy."

"Thank you, ma'am." I stood, stretching muscles that were already telling me I'd overdone it. "I'll finish the trim tomorrow, but we can move our bed back in now, so we won't have to sleep on the lanai."

She slid her arms around my waist and then pulled back, nose twitching. "You're a little…moist."

"That's honest sweat, Mrs. Murgasson."

"It is, and I would never criticize."

"I will shower before we go out to find ourselves some dinner. No sense exposing the rest of the world to my odiferousness."

"Is that a real word?"

"I doubt it, but like Shakespeare, I reserve the right to invent a *bon mot* when the need arises."

"How about my personal favorite, Eddie Poe? You've got to appreciate a guy who comes up with a word like tintinnabulation."

"'...of the bells, bells, bells, bells, bells, bells, bells.'"

We're aware that people often roll their eyes when we quote lines of poetry or snatches of timeless prose to each other, but it works for us. I spent my working years as an English professor at a small college in Montana. Alice read classic literature to distract herself from a horrible first marriage. Our mutual love of language helps to bring us closer, so the Madding Crowd can think whatever they choose.

Chapter Ten

Wilma (Earl and Wilma) Wednesday, 2:00 p.m.

Wednesday afternoon choir practice is one of my favorite times of the week. Rehearsal is relaxed, with people joking around and laughing a lot. I have to admit that it's nice to be noticed too. I'm often told what a nice voice I have, and though all the glory goes to God, I like that my voice pleases listeners. I don't think the Lord minds a person enjoying a compliment, as long as she doesn't get all big-headed about it.

Ronda, the choir director, handed out a number that had a soprano/tenor duet, and she put me and Del Hanna on it. She had it slated for March, so we ran through it a couple of times to get a feel for how it should go and then went on to other pieces.

When practice was over Del approached me, his handsome face friendly for once. "Can you stay a few minutes and go through the new duet?" That surprised me. Usually Del gets all huffy when he isn't the one and only star, and I'd half-expected him to suggest the selection would work better with only one voice, his.

Though I've never had much use for Del, he's one of God's children, so I was polite and said I could.

He asked our elderly pianist, Anita, to play the piece, and we sang it through once. "You and I have a very good blend," Del said when we finished. "It's going to be very effective."

That was the nicest thing he'd ever said to me. Though I try not to judge others, I'd chalked his kind of frosty attitude down to jealousy, since I'm asked to solo as often as he is. I wondered what had happened to change Del's attitude.

We sang the section through again, figuring out where we should breathe and when we should increase or decrease the volume. After that, Anita said she had to go.

When she'd packed up her music and left, Del sat down at the piano. "Would you like to hear your part all by itself?" he asked.

Though I never had any formal training, I'm pretty good at reading music, having played in the band at school as a kid. I know the notes, and I've got a good ear. Still, since Del was being nice, I said, "Sure."

He played the tune with one finger while I sang. Then he did it again, playing both parts and singing along. Finally he played the accompaniment, which surprised me. "I didn't realize you were such a good pianist," I said when we finished.

"I had a band, back in the day." He shrugged. "I don't mention it, because if people know you can play, they stick you with being the accompanist all the time. I much prefer singing to sitting behind the piano and being ignored."

I pictured Del in a '60s band. He'd probably been popular, since he looked a little like Mark Lindsay from Paul Revere and the Raiders. "Did you grow your hair long and wear fancy costumes?"

"I had a Fu Manchu and really long sideburns." He grinned. "We were awesome, at least in our own minds."

I wondered if Del formed his ideas about women during those days. The term *ladies' man* might have been invented for him, as long as the definition didn't include respect for the ladies' intelligence.

That reminded me, and I asked politely, "How does…Shawna

like living at B-Bird?"

"Not much." His tone closed the topic like the lid of a feed bin slapping down. "Shall we go through the song again?"

"I think I've got it."

His gaze met mine. "You certainly do, Wilma."

I felt my face warm, which meant my cheeks were turning bright red. "Um, thanks." Gathering my music I said, "I should be going. Earl worries if I don't get home soon after practice ends."

Del's eyes sparkled with humor. "Is he afraid someone's going to steal you away from him?"

"Oh, no," I responded. "We've been married too long to worry about that happening."

"Sometimes after years with the same man, a woman starts to wonder what she's missed." He paused. "She might get interested in experimenting a little."

"Not if she's a good person." Grabbing my purse from the chair I hurried outside, where the sun was hot but the situation was cooler.

Chapter Eleven

Al (Al & Karen) Wednesday 4:30 p.m.

While Karen was inside making dinner, Ron came by to let me know the other guys had agreed to investigate the cold case we'd been asked to look into. He said Alice was as excited about it as Julie was, which meant it was time for me to tell Karen.

When I went inside, all I could see of my wife was her rear end. While the casserole she'd made from last night's leftovers baked, Karen was cleaning out the refrigerator. I swallowed a grunt of irritation. While I get that a trailer is small and you have to limit what you keep, my wife makes culling food an art form. I have to hold on to items I want with both hands.

A jar of pickles sat on the counter. "Don't throw away my kosher dills."

"They've been in there for a month."

"They're pickles, Karen. They last a while."

"But you're not eating them."

"I will. Give me time."

Reluctantly, she put the jar back onto a door shelf. When she put a hand on a bowl of leftover scalloped potatoes I said, "I'll have those for lunch tomorrow."

She frowned at the new monkey wrench I'd tossed into her plans. "I was going to make you a grilled cheese sandwich tomorrow and use up this cheddar." Karen usually skips lunch because she thinks she's overweight.

"The cheese will last another day. I'll eat the potatoes tomorrow and have grilled cheese on Friday."

Pursing her lips, she pushed the bowl aside. "What about this salsa? Are you going to eat the little bit that's left in the jar?"

"I opened a new jar."

Her face appeared over the refrigerator door. "Why?"

"There wasn't enough in that jar, so I opened the new one."

Silence indicated that was the wrong answer, so I didn't object when she threw it into the trash. I'd have mixed the two once there was room in the second jar, but it wasn't worth arguing about.

"You know, Al," she said as she set several plates on the counter, "not everything in the fridge has to be on the top shelf."

"I like stuff where I can see it."

"But when it's all crowded together, you can't tell what's there." She moved some lunch meat and a loaf of bread to the bottom shelf. "The tall shelf is only for tall stuff, like milk jugs and pop bottles."

Since Karen does the lion's share of the work around our place, I promised myself I'd try to remember to do it the way she wants. Still, I don't get why a guy can't set stuff where he doesn't have to bend over to get at it.

"That cop that investigated the murder last month came to see Ron and Julie," I said as Karen opened a jar of mayonnaise and sniffed it. "They're looking for a guy that might be living at B-Bird under an assumed name."

She stopped rearranging and closed the refrigerator door. "Really."

"Yeah. He wants some of us to do a secret canvass to find out who it might be." I explained what I knew of the case, adding that Ron had gotten permission from the detective to include us as helpers.

She was every bit as skeptical as I'd feared. "You're telling me the police want a bunch of senior citizens to do a secret investigation."

"Ron thinks they don't expect to get a result," I said honestly. "He guesses somebody up in Nashville never forgot the murders, maybe a cop who hates that his first case never got solved. The people at our P.D. want to be able to tell their fellow officers they made an honest attempt to find the guy, but they doubt it's going to happen."

Karen's nose wrinkled. "How would we go about looking for this mystery man?"

"Ron says we'll sit down together tomorrow and figure that out."

In spite of herself, Karen was interested. "One of us could say we had relatives living up there at the time."

"But wouldn't that make whoever killed them clam up like a…" I couldn't come up with anything except, "...clam?"

"Maybe, but we'd watch how the suspect reacts when we mention the murders. A guilty person would show some sign of nervousness."

Karen's use of the word suspect told me she'd come over to my side. It seemed she might need a distraction from medical bills and doctor appointments as much as I did.

We talked all through supper about how we might judge a guy's reaction. Our ideas ranged from practical to ridiculous, and it felt kind of like a game. At several points one of us said aloud that this was serious, not merely a diversion for old people. Still, for once there was a new, intriguing topic of conversation. Not the weather, not the date of my next blood test, and not how fast I should finish off a jar of kosher dills.

Chapter Twelve

Tommy (Tommy & Alice) Wednesday, 7:00 p.m.

For a guy who's into DIY home renovation, life in a trailer can be a trial. Pretty much everything is fake: the wood isn't wood; the tile isn't tile. Materials are so lightweight there's not much to nail to. Screws often aren't anchored to anything, and behind the visible facade you're liable to encounter odds and ends that don't match and aren't the best quality. Though I do a lot of projects to spruce our place up, I'm aware that I'm putting lipstick on a pig.

My most recent job was replacing the ancient carpeting in our bedroom with wood flooring. I made sure I got most of the work done in one day, since the lanai can get mighty cold on January nights. Though I got the flooring laid, I came up short on trim boards and energy around three, so I quit for the day. After dinner with Alice at a pizza place we like, I walked down to the woodshop to see what there was for scraps. I only needed a few short pieces, and since the amount the lumber company charges is criminal, I figured I'd make what I needed to finish the job.

Because the night was beyond chilly, there weren't many people out. I passed a man bundled up like Jeremiah Johnson and a woman looking hunched and unhappy as she walked her dog, a doggy-doo bag protruding from her coat pocket. The dog wanted to check me out, but his human gave an impatient tug on the leash, and they went on.

Seeing them made me think about complaints lodged at the last council meeting. When people live in a confined space, disagreements are bound to crop up. At B-Bird, animals are a big point of contention. Do we want them or not? What limits should be set? Who's responsible for seeing that the rules are obeyed? Current park policy allows small dogs, but we'd recently had to fine-tune the language, since a few residents stretched the definition of small. Now the contract says "under twenty pounds," which can still be a problem. A five-pound puppy can grow to be far over that limit from one year to the next.

Cats are allowed with the understanding that they're kept inside or on a leash. That rule is unpopular with some of the cat owners and most of the cats. Felines are hunters and wanderers, and they often slip outdoors without permission from their owners.

Our neighbor Donna had an experience, and she tells the story on herself with great amusement. She and her husband were sitting on their porch late one night. Since it was cool, they turned their space heater on. In the middle of a comment, Ken suddenly stopped short and said, "Donna, there are eyes under your chair."

Donna took one look, let out a screech, and bolted for the house. "Come back," Ken called a moment later. "It's just a cat looking to get warm."

"I can't come back yet," she called from inside the trailer. "I was pretty scared, so I need to put on clean underwear."

As I smiled to myself at the story, I noticed a guy ahead of me. Though I couldn't see him well, I got the sense that he was young. He had a stealthy look about him, and George's report came to mind. I quickened my pace, thinking I'd catch up, start a conversation, and establish whether he belonged at B-Bird.

I was about ten feet behind when the scrape of my shoe on the pavement alerted the stranger to my presence. He turned enough to see me, though not enough for me to get a look at his face, which was obscured by a hood. He quickened his steps.

Not sure whether it was wise or not I called out, "Can I ask what you're doing in the park?"

His response was to move faster. I picked up my pace again. He might be a visitor, but he wasn't acting like someone who had a reason to be on the property. Intruders aren't unheard of at B-Bird. We've had some bicycles stolen, since almost no one has a place to store theirs inside. We'd also had incidents where unlocked cars were ransacked for change and items that could easily be sold. Like a lot of residents, I lock my car, chain our bikes to a carport post at night, and installed a motion light, hoping its sudden, bright glow will send any prospective thief scuttling for the shadows.

Instinct told me the guy I was following was up to no good. I could have gone home and called the cops, but I was curious to see where he was headed, so I stayed behind him.

He approached my original destination, the wood shop. The large, barn-like structure has a staple-and-hasp latch on the door. It's got a padlock, meant to keep strangers out of our tools and lumber supply. Everyone in the park knows the combination (B-Bird's street number, 4332), but most people leave the padlock hanging on a nail above the latch. You arrive with an armload of wood, and it's a nuisance to have to set it down, open the padlock, and set it aside. We give up a little security for our convenience.

At the back of the building, a sliding door leads to a fenced outside area where guys can work on larger projects. The gate there also has a padlock, and it has the same combination. The gate is left unlocked as well. As one guy put it, "Who's going to come in here and steal the birdhouse you're making for your sister's back yard?"

I was surprised when the intruder ducked into the wood shop, but I guessed he intended to lock me out. There was no way he could do that, as he'd soon see. Imagining his frustration, I opened the door and flipped the light switch. Before me were a half-dozen workstations with band saws, grinders, lathes, and other power tools bolted to cabinet bases. Each base was large enough to hide a man, and I imagined my quarry crouched behind one of them, hoping I'd take a look and move on. "I don't mean to harass you, kid," I called, "but this is private property. You need to be on your way."

My answer was the grind of the sliding door at the back opening. He'd gone outside rather than face me, which was okay. I'd had my say, and if he was smart, he'd continue through the gate, leave the park, and not come back.

I listened for a few seconds, heard scrabbling at the back, and then silence. Almost certain he was gone but not quite, I moved cautiously to the rear door, which he'd left open. Exiting the building, I passed through the outdoor workspace, lit by a motion-activated light, and pushed on the wooden gate. When it didn't open, I realized the kid had padlocked it so I couldn't continue chasing him. That was okay too, since I'd already decided not to. Turning, I went back inside, closed the slider, and headed to the scrap bin. With a little rummaging, I found some boards I could rip to make the trim I needed. As I set them under my arm, a metallic clunk sounded at the front door. It took me a second to realize it was the padlock sliding into place. The little jerk had locked me in.

I hurried to the front door and pushed on it. When it didn't open, I went back outside and re-tried the gate. Of course it didn't budge either. I returned to the front door and tried it again, like a child refusing to accept the limits of his playpen. Finally, I recognized reality. Neither padlock was going to magically open and let me out.

What, then?

The place was cold and getting colder. I could probably break the lock on the fence gate if I ran at it a few times, but I was reluctant to do that. I wasn't thrilled with admitting some punk had got the better of me, and I imagined my neighbors having a laugh at my expense. "A guy can have all kinds of degrees and still be dumb," Big-mouth Del would probably say, and I'd have no answer for it.

Pressing the rough wood tentatively, I considered anonymity. Who would know it was me who'd done it? Alice knew where I'd gone, but if I asked her not to, she wouldn't rat me out. I still hesitated to take that step. I didn't want to wreck the door, and the resulting noise might bring someone to investigate. My anonymity would be gone.

As one does when wondering what to do next, I glanced up. Stars twinkled overhead, and I realized I was looking through a gap. The pitched roof of the shop sat over open gable ends, left that way to allow air circulation, for cooling and to dispel sawdust. If I could scale the wall, I could climb out through the gap, let myself down the other side, and walk away free.

To do that, I had to get my hands on a header four feet over my head. That meant I needed a boost, so I started gathering lumber, setting the bigger pieces down first and adding height with smaller ones. The result wasn't exactly a secure platform, but by using the wall to steady myself, I was able to climb to the top of the pile. Stretching, I reached up, caught the header, and pulled myself up, bracing my feet on the corrugated metal wall. It wasn't quiet, and when my weight left the stacked lumber, pieces skittered off, sounding like scattered Tinkertoys and leaving a puzzle for whoever came in first tomorrow morning.

That was when I realized I'm not as young as I once was. It took every bit of strength I had to pull myself up onto the header. Once there, I sat for a few seconds to get my wind back. When I felt somewhat revived, I pulled my legs up, turned my body, and started lowering myself down. There wasn't much to hold onto, and my arms aren't as strong as they once were, so my exit was anything but graceful. The sleeve of my shirt caught on a nail-head and gave way with a long ripping sound. Worse, once my full weight was suspended from my hands, they slipped off the beam. With a suppressed yelp of pain and frustration, I dropped unceremoniously to the ground. After stumbling a few steps to keep from falling on my rear, I recovered.

Despite all that, I was pleased with myself. I'd made it down safely, and the only casualties were three scraped fingers and a torn shirt. Going to the padlock, I opened it, undid the hasp, reached inside, and turned off the lights. I'd bested the now-absent intruder, escaping the trap he'd sprung. No one saw my clumsy descent. No one heard the undignified sounds I'd made upon landing. I was feeling like a pretty lucky guy.

My mood was squashed when the Astaire sisters came into view, no doubt returning home from mid-week prayer service. Elsie and Chelsie see themselves as the park's wise elders, dispensing advice on anything and everything with a certainty you couldn't dent with a Sherman tank. They saw it as their duty to comment on anything that wasn't "right," not in terms of gossip so much as in terms of object lessons: Your failings were passed on to others so they might not fail in similar ways.

As they tripped toward me, their steps tiny, like goats on pavement, I knew I was in for an interrogation. I stood in a spill of light, my hair coated with cobweb, my hands dirty and bloody, and my sleeve almost separated from my flannel jacket. Seeing me there, they stopped, peering forward until they recognized me. Reassured, they came on, but then, they noticed the state I was in. "Mr. Murgasson." Elsie's voice was even more disapproving than usual. "You've ruined your shirt."

"Yes, I was…woodworking, and I caught it on…something."

Coming closer, she examined the damage. "You've torn the fabric itself. That can't be repaired."

"Well, it's pretty old anyway."

"You should buy better quality." She sniffed. "Canada makes

the best flannel shirts."

"Father always chose Canadian flannel," Chelsie put in helpfully.

"I'm sure that's true. I'll have a look online."

Elsie reared back as if I'd cursed. "Doesn't your wife do the shopping? Surely, as an experienced homemaker, she knows better than you which fabrics are most durable."

Since all I wanted was to get away, I said, "Of course. I'll ask Alice to help me out."

That satisfied Elsie, at least as much as she's ever satisfied. "Good evening, then, Mr. Murgasson."

Holding my tattered sleeve, I backed away. "Have a nice night, ladies."

Chapter Thirteen

Karen (Al & Karen) Wednesday, 7:30 p.m.

Al had gone in to watch TV. I sat outside, having my last cigarette of the day, though it was cold enough that I turned on the heater to warm my feet. I was thinking about our kids, who never seem to get their acts together. The oldest moves from job to job all the time, always unhappy with how "they" treat him. I mention, as gently as possible, that constantly shifting jobs looks bad on an application, but he insists I'm old-fashioned. "People have lots of jobs over their lifetime now," he'll argue. "It's not like when Dad hired on at the plant and stayed for forty years." He might be right, I don't know, but I can't believe the next job will be better simply because it's new.

My younger son is the opposite of his brother. He works at a place where they treat him like dirt, but he never looks for something better. "It's not so bad," he'll say, but his wife tells me what he puts up with: the ever-changing schedule, getting sent home halfway through a shift because business is slow, expected to come in on short notice to cover those who call in sick, and unsafe working conditions. I often wish I could give a little of my first-born's confidence to the second one, and some of my baby's humility to his elder brother.

The night had quieted around me. Most B-Bird residents are in by dark, so few cars went by, and the night was cool enough that not many walkers were out. As I stubbed out my cigarette and rose to go inside, a figure passed under the street lamp a few yards down from our lot. He moved at a dead run, which led me to conclude it wasn't a resident. Most of us are too old to be in that much of a hurry, unless maybe our shoes are on fire.

For a few seconds I was…not scared, really, but alert. Only the day before, one of the women at the meeting hall had insisted a man followed her down Cormorant Street, staying twenty feet back no matter how slow or fast she walked. Alice, who'd been with me at the time, rolled her eyes, suggesting she thought the woman was exaggerating.

I waited to see what would happen next. Was someone being chased? No one else showed up. No one screamed. No one shouted, "Stop, thief!"

A minute later I heard a car start up at the end of the street.

A visitor had cut between trailers to get to his car. The practice is discouraged by park management, but that doesn't stop people from doing it, day or night. Rumors were making us all nervous, but there wasn't anything to worry about. No one had reported anything missing for months, and despite Al's fussing, I wasn't all that concerned about the Peeping Tom everyone was upset about. Surely if there was one, he'd get bored with watching senior citizens watch TV and move on.

Making sure my cigarette butt was completely extinguished, I went into the trailer and forgot about it.

Chapter Fourteen

Wilma (Earl & Wilma) Thursday, 1:00 a.m.- Thursday, 1:00 p.m.

When Earl told me Ron wanted us to help Officer O'Connor find a man named Greg Miles, I didn't say at first what I thought of the idea, but it seemed wrong. Catching murderers is important, but so is friendship. To do what Ron proposed, we'd be forced to lie to the people at B-Bird. Tommy had already said yes and so had Al, which made Earl unwilling to say no. "Ron didn't want to leave us out," he said, "but I told him it's up to you."

Late at night, when we're probably the only two awake in the park, we talk, often about being a good person and doing what God wants you to do with your life. That night, even though Earl didn't criticize anyone, I realized he wasn't as excited about playing amateur detective as the others were. "I don't like the idea of fooling people into telling us things," he said, fiddling with the volume on the radio. "I'm no kind of detective. I'm afraid I'll stutter and stammer and embarrass myself."

"Maybe you and me could work together on it. I mean, if we decide we want to join in."

Earl's face brightened. "That might help. You could bring up how we met, and I could chime in and keep it going, about the sixties and where we were and stuff like that."

"Except it will be dishonest. I'm not sure how I feel about that."

Several times we drifted away from the subject, unable to make a decision, but it kept coming up again. One or the other would mention it, and we'd repeat the good and bad parts of the plan. After a while we'd talk about something else or sit in silence, watching the moon make its way above the trailers across the street. Finally Earl said, "Ron and Julie are really smart. They know what they're doing."

"Does that mean you want to join in with them?"

"I think it's our duty to help the police," Earl replied. "It'll be hard, lying to people, but murder's worse than a fib or two."

The eight of us met at Al and Karen's the next afternoon. Julie brought her laptop, and she'd used the park directory to make a list of all the residents. On what she called a spreadsheet, she could manipulate the information all kinds of ways. She'd already eliminated the women, though Alice joked the killer could have had a sex-change operation. Al said that was quite a lot to give up, even to escape murder charges.

"He deserves to get away with murder if he went that far," Karen said. I was embarrassed by the whole idea of a person changing sexes, but Alice laughed. "You gotta admit it's the perfect disguise."

Since nobody actually believed that was the case, we went back to the spreadsheet. "I tried to separate the men by age," Julie said, "but I had to make some guesses. Greg Miles was somewhere between twenty and thirty in 1967, which means he's between seventy-three and eighty-three now."

"Then we can eliminate all the men over eighty-five and under seventy," Alice said.

Julie's brow furrowed. "I could be more accurate if I had exact birth dates."

"I might be able to get them," Karen said. "Marlene in the office has a birthday list, and she knows what we're up to, since she and Detective O'Connor are dating. I don't think her sharing it with us would violate anyone's privacy."

"Great." Julie scrolled to the final page. "Right now I've got a hundred and eighty-eight names."

"Less four," Tommy said, circling a finger to indicate the guys at the table.

"I took you guys out first thing," Julie said. "I also removed obvious ones, like Tom Haines, who has that purple birthmark on his face. That would have been mentioned in the description." She laid out sheets of printed information. "Here's who we have so far."

As we scanned the list, we tried to eliminate men that one of us knew or knew about. Tommy pointed out that Jeb Daniels was missing two fingers, but Ron said we had no way of knowing when he'd lost them. Another man has a pronounced widow's peak, which Alice said seemed like something that would have been mentioned in the description.

"The hairstyles back then might have hidden it," Al said. "A lot of guys were copying the Beatles." Running a hand over his buzzed hair he added in a comical manner, "Me, I had the Elvis look back then."

Julie claimed it was doubtful anyone from Canada was Greg Miles. "It's not impossible," Alice noted. "Truckers cross from Canada every day, and they probably did then too."

Ron made a suggestion. "Let's start with U.S. citizens and revisit the Canadians if our initial efforts don't pan out."

After a lot of back and forth, we ended up eliminating, or at least setting on the back burner, fifty-three residents. Julie sat back from her laptop, pleased with what we'd accomplished. "That means we each get seventeen men to interview."

I glanced at Earl, who'd found something on his thumbnail that seemed to fascinate him. Were we really going to agree to this? When he stayed quiet, I figured we were.

"I'll take the four who sing in the choir," I said. "And any others I already know." Meeting Julie's gaze I added, "I don't feel comfortable striking up a fake conversation with a man I've never spoken to before. I would never give a man the idea I find him…attractive or whatever."

"That's fine, Wilma," Alice said. "You and Earl pick first, and we'll figure out the rest."

That was a relief, and I was grateful to Alice. Though she's a very confident person, she seems to understand that not everyone is that way. I took the pencil Julie provided and put a *W* beside the names of men I knew well enough to talk to. Most of them were from church, which meant they weren't likely to be murderers anyway. I passed the list to Earl, and he chose his seventeen. Ron said Al should go next, since he isn't very mobile, but he had no trouble choosing. Almost everyone who walks down Osprey Street knows Al, and a lot of them stop to chat with him as they pass. Karen chose men who live fairly close to her and Al, probably because she doesn't like leaving him alone for too long at a time. The man gets more fragile every day, and she watches over him like he's made of glass.

Tommy and Alice chose next, and Julie and Ron got the leftovers, people none of us knew much about. Some residents don't socialize with anyone, and a few are seldom seen outside their trailers. When Alice commented that they had the hardest job, Julie replied. "It'll be fun. You never know what we'll find when you meet someone new."

We left with Julie's promise that we'd each have our own list the next day with names and lot numbers. It was up to each of us to figure out how to bring up the subject of where the man was in July of 1967.

Earl and me walked down Osprey and then turned onto Main to head home to Hawk Street. The day was cool but not too bad, and we stopped at the lake to watch the birds for a while. They poked along the shore with their long, skinny beaks, looking for whatever it is they call supper. The lake was quiet, and behind us were muted sounds: a door closing, a TV turned up for a resident who apparently didn't hear well, a car out on the highway taking off from a stoplight like a jet airplane. Earl stared across the water, enjoying what he calls his "nature fix."

Usually I feel refreshed in such moments too, but today I was too antsy to find the view restful. "I don't know if I like this."

"I've been thinking about it." Earl turned to me, his face crumpled with concern. "I think I should take your list along with mine. Ron says it isn't dangerous, but if we find this man and he thinks he's cornered, who knows what he'll do? You could get hurt."

I almost groaned out loud. I was worried about offending people and God by being a snoop, and Earl was imagining me getting clubbed over the head by some eighty-year-old. "That's not why I don't like it."

"But it's true," he argued. "It could be dangerous, so I'm going to tell them to leave you out of it."

I tried to keep my voice level. "It's okay for Karen, Alice, and Julie to investigate but not me?"

"They'll do what they want. You're my wife, and my job is taking care of you."

Suddenly, my doubts about the project were overcome by irritation. “We’ll ask a few questions, Earl. I won’t curl up and die from it.”

He seemed confused, and to be honest, I was confused too, but Earl thinking I couldn’t do something my friends were perfectly able to do made me angry. “I’ll do my part,” I said. For the first time since the project was raised, I was one hundred percent committed. “I’ll do my part, and I’ll be fine.”

Chapter Fifteen

Karen (Al & Karen) Thursday, 2:30 p.m.

I stopped at the office Thursday afternoon to ask for a copy of the birthday list and found Marlene, the secretary, trying to assist Larry, one of our oldest residents. I stood back, waiting until she finished with him, but after a while I realized it wouldn't be quick.

Larry apparently had an appointment with an eye doctor. As he explained with disjointed sentences and a voice loud enough for a wind tunnel, I learned that he didn't know where the office was, what the practice was called, or the name of the doctor. Though Marlene was patient, I felt her frustration. Larry had brought a phone book, and he asked her to read him the list of ophthalmologists so he'd hear a name that sounded familiar. She pointed out, very gently, that the book was from 2010 and covered Miami and its suburbs.

"Call the coffee shop down on the corner," Larry ordered. "Some of the guys there know the doc's name, because they helped me make the appointment."

Obligingly, Marlene found the number and called Dorie's Diner. By now I was hooked. Putting a pod in the coffeemaker, I listened as she spoke with three different people. Finally, someone who knew Larry suggested his buddy Anton was likely to know the answer. Setting the phone against her chest Marlene said, "Anton isn't there right now. Can we call him?"

Larry looked at her as if she'd asked for a slice of the moon. "I don't know his other name. Just Anton."

Marlene spoke again to the waitress. "Is there anyone else there who has coffee with Larry?"

She tried Charlie, who seemed willing to help but had no idea Larry was experiencing eye trouble. He apparently told Marlene all about his own cataracts, and she waited until she could get a word in to ask if anyone else there might be able to help. That led her to Milburn, whose voice carried well enough that I heard every word. "Larry? Sure, I know Larry."

"Well, he's here in my office and—"

"Tell him to get his butt down here. Nobody to play gin rummy with."

"He's trying to figure out when his eye appointment is. He thinks it might be today."

"Eyes, huh? I got pretty good eyes for my age. Can't hear a damned thing, though."

Marlene glanced skyward, as if praying. "Do you know who the doctor is?"

"Which doctor?"

"The doctor Larry's supposed to see for his eyes." I had to hand it to Marlene, whose tone revealed no frustration.

"Can't say I do. Anton says he's tall. Used to play round-ball."

"That's right," Larry chimed in. "He got drafted by the Celtics but didn't make the cut."

He remembered which NBA team the guy didn't make but not his name?

As Marlene ended the call, a little signal went off in my brain. "Could they mean Dr. Zebic? Al saw him last year when he tore his cornea, and he’s very tall.”

“That’s him,” Larry crowed. “Zebic. Anton says he’s the best because he’s a Serb, like him.”

“Great,” Marlene said. “You can call his office and find out when your appointment is.”

Larry gave an embarrassed cough. “I can't see to dial a phone. Anton did the calling and gave ’em my information.” He leaned on the counter. “I got that General Motors insurance, you know? It’s pretty good stuff.”

“Anton made the appointment.”

“Yeah. It was either the twentieth of January or the twentieth of February.” After a pause he added, “Or maybe the thirtieth.”

“Let’s see what I can find out.” Marlene looked up the office number online and called. “I’m here with Larry Finnegan, and he’s forgotten the date of his appointment with Doctor Zebic.” After a brief wait, she wrote the information in large block letters on a sheet of legal paper, thanked the person on the other end, and ended the call. Handing him the note she said, “Your appointment is for Monday, Larry, January 20th, at 10:00 a.m.”

“Good, good. Thanks for the help.” He turned away. “Not sure how I’ll get there.”

Marlene caught my eye and rolled hers, but only a little. “You don’t have a ride?”

“How could I ask for a ride when I didn’t know the day?”

“But there’s someone who’ll take you, right?”

“Well, Ted, my neighbor, usually drives me, but he’s up north in Gainesville visiting his sister.” He frowned. “That kid on Gull

Street gives people rides sometimes."

"He does, but he's Uber. Can you pay the fee?"

Larry scratched at his uneven, gray whiskers. "Maybe I'll walk out to the road and catch the bus."

With a disturbing mental image of Larry wandering across six lanes of traffic, lost and half-blind, I spoke up. "Al and I can take you."

He turned to peer at me. "Al? Who's Al?"

"The guy on Osprey Street who sits on his porch all day."

"Oh, sure. Al." He showed his dentures in a big grin. "Good guy."

"He likes going for rides, so we'll take you to Dr. Zebic's office." That wasn't completely true. Al and I both hate Florida traffic, and ten a.m. is a terrible time to venture out on the roads. Since Al is a bucket of broken pieces these days, I'd get to do the driving. I'm getting used to it, and it was a good deed for a fellow resident.

"That's real nice of you," Larry said. "When I got the sugar diabeetus, I gave my old Chevy to my granddaughter." After a pause he said, "Now who are you again?"

"Karen." I added the term most at B-Bird method know me by. "Karen from Pittsburg."

When Larry had shuffled his way out the door, Marlene and I were alone in the office. We come from the same town in northern Lower Michigan, though we lived there forty years apart, so we chatted a little about home first. Then I asked about the birthday list. "Sure thing," she said. "Ray told me you're helping out." As she spoke, she located it in her files and sent it to the printer.

"How are things with you and Detective O'Connor going?"

Her smile said it all. "Really good. I think we'll be getting a place together soon."

As I took the list, Marlene thanked me for offering to help Larry. "I worry about him, but it's not like we have a car service for the residents who can't or shouldn't drive."

"We have to watch out for each other," I said. "If we live long enough, we'll all be like Larry someday."

"No way," she responded. "I couldn't deal."

I left, thinking that although Marlene was sympathetic, she didn't understand what aging is like. When you're thirty-something, it's hard to imagine you'll ever be completely dependent on the kindness of others.

Chapter Sixteen

Al (Al & Karen) Thursday

I started my part of the investigation right away, even though we didn't have official lists yet. I remembered who'd I'd picked to interview, and most of them passed by every day around the same time.

I'd been up since four, since every way I tried to lie in bed made something hurt. Not wanting to wake Karen, I'd got up quietly, gone outside, turned on the heater, and lit my first cigarette of the day. If I can get out without her hearing me, she'll sometimes sleep until five.

The first few hours were quiet, but around daylight I started seeing walkers. The serious ones wear earbuds and stride right by, too intent on exercise to be sociable. Others, more laid back about their heart rate and all that, stop to talk. Some even sit for a while, sharing stories about yesterday or yesteryear. The men I'd chosen from Julie's list were that kind, likely to stop, if not today then within a week or so.

The first guy I talked to was Wayne from Crane Street. I heard him before I saw him, since he converses almost non-stop with his walking companion. "Behave yourself, Angus, or the next time we pass by the adoption place, I'm dropping you off."

He didn't get an answer, and I didn't expect he would, since Angus is a dog. Wayne seems to go a little slower each week, but he keeps it up, and I give him credit for trying. The dog has much younger legs and not much self-control, so they carry on a running feud about how fast the pace should be. The dog pulls at his harness.

Wayne pulls back. The dog slows for a few seconds before he strains to hurry ahead again.

When Wayne slipped the loop of Angus' leash over our porch post, climbed the steps, and sank into a chair, I surmised that dog-walking is getting to be too much for him. His breath whistled through his nostrils, and a faint sheen of sweat showed on his brow. Angus followed him up the steps, sniffing in the corners. Wayne growled a command to sit, but Angus took his sweet time before obeying.

"Nice morning," I said.

"It didn't get as cold last night as it did the one before. I'd have stayed in until it got warmer, but Angus here had other ideas."

"Pets do like to be the boss."

"I try to teach him things, like when to be quiet and how to behave in public. But Ginger spoils him rotten, so anything I try to do gets me nowhere." His frown might have been irritation, might have been near-sightedness. "I'll tell you something, Al. Pets are like kids. You have to teach them how to act so they'll be welcome when they go out into the world." Glaring down at Angus he went on, "If you let them be brats, nobody wants to be around them."

"You aren't wrong there."

Wayne sniffed a couple of times, something he does a lot. I suspected allergies and hoped it wasn't to dog dander. "Ginger was a good mother to our kids, but now?" He shook his head. "She spoils this little guy rotten." He paused, chewing at his lip. "I don't fight with her about it though. Angus is all we've got to care about these days."

"Are you interested in a cup of coffee?"

"No thanks. Can't have sugar, which makes coffee undrinkable as far as I'm concerned. I'm not supposed to have caffeine either." He ended with the old joke: "I'm at the age where if I put something in my mouth and it tastes good, the docs want me to spit it out."

I saw an opening. "How old are you, anyway?"

"Eighty-one next month."

"I suppose you've been around lots of cities, huh?"

He frowned at the question. "Sure. Why do you ask?"

I felt my ears start to burn. I couldn't remember the last time I deliberately lied to someone, and one of the good things about getting old is being able to be honest. No boss to please, no girls to impress, no stud-muffin friends to compare yourself to. You say what you think or you keep your mouth shut.

Still, I had to follow through. "Karen and I were talking last night about some relatives of hers that used to live in Nashville." I stopped. "You ever been there?"

"Yeah," Wayne said. "I lived there after high school."

Could I be so lucky as to find our target on the first try? "When was that?"

His brow knitted briefly. "Well, I graduated in '57, so I was there from then until 1960. Is that when your people lived there?"

"No. They were there in '67."

Wayne nodded. "By then I was in Ohio. All my life, I worked for Kroger, and they gave me my own store up in Sunbury in '64." After a pause he added, "They'd give you a pin for every ten years of service. I still got all five of mine."

As Wayne talked about his old job, I realized I had no way of knowing if what he said was true. Were we going to take these men's word for it when they said where they were in '67? If so, the whole project seemed pointless.

Ten minutes later, Wayne limped down my steps and went on, muttering at Angus to slow down and go straight. Karen came outside, sat down opposite me, and lit a cigarette. "I heard most of that. Do you think we can cross him off the list?"

"It would be nice if we could confirm it somehow."

"Ask Ginger, maybe?"

I shook my head. "I say we give the information to that cop and let him decide what needs more investigation."

Later that day, Karen talked to Julie about it. "She thinks she can check the information on the store's website," she reported, "though she's not sure if there'll be information on managers from that far back."

"That's good. The more people we eliminate entirely, the easier it will be for the cops to zero in on who's left."

"We'll consider Wayne a question mark," Karen said. "The rest will be up to Julie."

"She's going to be busy for a long time if she tries to check everybody's story." I grinned, adding, "Lucky for me, I can't help. Don't have a clue how to turn on a computer."

"If you were a true product of the '60s you'd know the answer to that," Karen said. "You say, 'I love you, computer' and that turns it on."

Chapter Seventeen

Ron (Ron & Julie) Friday, 8:00 a.m.

Using the birthday list Karen fetched from the office, Julie eliminated four and added two residents to the list of men who might be Greg Miles. By ten o'clock on Friday, she had eight neat lists printed and ready to go. Each had the man's name and lot number, followed by a space to make notes after the interview. At the right margin was a box we'd check when we all agreed a guy was clear of suspicion.

I was eager to get to work on my list. It's good to have things to occupy your mind as you get older, because I sure don't want to get dementia. I'd been trying to come up with ways to meet guys I've lived in the same park with for years but never spoken to, except maybe to say "Excuse me" as we pass at some event. Some of them I knew by sight. A few I'd have sworn I'd never heard of before. How did I miss that we have a guy at B-Bird named Harry Longbaugh? I loved Butch Cassidy and the Sundance Kid, but I'd missed old Harry's name in the directory.

I thought the plan I devised would work. I'd knock on doors with a clipboard, assessing interest among residents for a slot-car racing club. The topic would appeal mostly to men, and it would give me a chance to talk about the good old days when the hobby was popular. I'd then steer the conversation to specifics, where the guy was living in the summer of '67.

A slot car club was something I'd been considering anyway. We have lots of outdoor activities for men at B-Bird, but not so many rainy-day things. I'd already scoped out a corner of the activity room where we could set up tracks. I didn't mind organizing the club, because as a kid I was crazy about those little cars. My dad and I built different tracks and raced our favorite cars against each other. The modern kits aren't cheap, but you work all your life to enjoy retirement, right?

In order to not be too obvious, I mixed people I know in with the ones targeted for our investigation. My neighbor Harry liked the idea right away. "It would be good to have something to do inside," he said when I explained my idea. "Otherwise you sit on your duff and watch reruns all day." When I approached the first person on my suspects list, I already had Harry and Tommy listed in the *Yes* column.

I knocked on the door of #20 Stork, and after a few seconds a grizzled face appeared at the screen. "Yeah?"

"Hi. I'm Ron Rogers from over on Egret Street, and I'm trying to find guys who might be interested in setting up a few slot-car tracks here in the park."

"Slot-cars?"

"Yeah, like in the '60s. It'll be fun to bring them back. We'd set up events every month or so. It would be great when the grandkids visit."

The man's face got smaller as his forehead, nose and mouth puckered. "Ain't got no grandkids."

"But you do remember slot-cars, right? I'm from Wisconsin, and they were big there."

"I remember a little."

"Where do you come from?"

"Why is that your business?"

This wasn't as easy as I'd imagined. "You don't sound like a Northerner."

The almost-toothless mouth twisted. "Born and raised right here in Florida."

"Wow. I don't meet many natives."

One eye opened from its squint. "Well, now you did."

"You ever live anywhere else?"

He stood a little straighter. "Never been more'n a hundred miles from Tampa Bay."

I'd learned what I came for. "If you're interested in the club, I can keep you informed."

"I work every day," he said dismissively. "Got no time for clubs and that."

"It was nice meeting you." It was a lie, but I had to say something.

I made it through six of my seventeen the first day, and I was pretty sure five of them couldn't be our guy. One was a possibility, but not a great one. He admitted to knowing Nashville a little but claimed he'd never driven anything bigger than a pickup truck.

Around three, when I retired to my carport and put ice on my knee, Hank stopped by on his bike. "You been awful busy," he observed. Self-appointed B-Bird head gossip, Hank can't rest until he knows what everybody's doing. Though he wasn't on my suspect list, I gave him the spiel about the slot-car track.

"Sounds like something a lot of guys would like."

"They have kits for semis too," I said, following my prepared script. "Big-rig events are popular at racetracks these days, and I was thinking we could have events for both." After a beat I said, "Did you ever drive a big rig, Hank?"

"Nope." He pushed his bike backwards into the street, turned the handlebars, and set his feet on the pedals. "Had a lot of jobs over my lifetime, but I never got into that."

As he rode away, my brain replayed a story, someone describing how loud it was in the cab of a semi back before modern improvements muffled the noise. The voice in my head sounded like Hank's rumbly bass, but it could have been a half-dozen other guys. I talk to so many people in the park that it's easy to mix up who said what.

Chapter Eighteen

Alice (Tommy & Alice) Friday, 1:00 p.m.

As I passed Karen and Al's place, she was pulling weeds from her flower bed with one hand and holding a cigarette in the other. Since she was alone, I stopped, leaned a hip against her golf cart, and asked softly, "How are your interviews going?"

"Slower than I expected. The two I caught up with seem innocent, but it took me most of the morning to find that out."

"What's your approach?"

"I cooked up a story about being related to the murdered couple. I steer the conversation to the crime, and I tell it like an episode of *Unsolved Mysteries.* Then I say, 'You mean you never heard about it? Where were you living back then, anyway?'"

"Smart. It's human nature to answer a direct question, even if the questioner doesn't have a good reason to ask."

"Exactly. Both men I spoke to answered." She wiped the sweat from her forehead with her sleeve. "The second guy looked at me kind of funny, like he wondered why it mattered."

I frowned. "I'm not sure we're going to get good information by simply asking for it. This guy has had years to build a cover story, so why would he blurt out, 'Yeah, I was in Nashville on the night two people got murdered'? Added to that, can you tell if someone's lying, especially someone you don't know well? I don't think I can."

Karen's practical streak counters Julie's optimism, and she said candidly, "Ron's pretty sure the cops don't expect us to find the guy. This is all about being able to tell their brother officers up in Nashville that they tried."

I sighed, admitting that was probably the case. "If I'm going to put forth effort, I'd like to think we have a shot at finding the guy."

Leaving Karen to her weeding, I went on to the library to return four books. Tommy reads mostly non-fiction, and I'm all over the place, depending on my mood. By Christmas we'd read everything the little library has to offer, so I was hoping something new and interesting had been donated in the last few days.

A man stood with his back to me when I entered, head tilted to one side as he perused the titles. When I realized it was Matthew Nowicki, I almost backed out the door. He turned when he heard the door open and, not wanting to be openly rude, I said, "Nice day out there."

A comment on the weather isn't usually controversial, but Matthew is possibly the world's biggest conspiracy theorist. "It is," he replied. "HAARP must have decided to let us have a few nice days before they hit us with whatever disaster comes next on their agenda." In his condescending, mansplaining way, he translated the acronym. "HARP is the High Frequency Active Auroral Research Program."

Something Tommy said buzzed through my brain. "I thought they closed that down."

One brow rose, and I was reminded of Vincent Price as whatever evil scientist you remember him playing. "That's what you were told."

"Hmm."

Apparently that response was too pale. Matthew took a step

toward me, his dark eyes flashing. "You know the government controls the weather, right? They have radio-technology that can bring on hurricanes like Katrina or huge earthquakes, like the one in Haiti."

Arguing against Matthew's nut-job claims does no good, but I couldn't stop myself from asking a question. "Why would they do that?"

"Think what a powerful weapon it will be once the system is perfected." He jabbed at his own head with a finger. "So far they're only testing, but who's going to stand up to the U.S. once we can send a tsunami their way, or a blizzard that lasts for weeks?" He cleared his throat. "Powerful weapon."

"You're saying our government practices on its own citizens?"

He shrugged. "You don't think Big Brother can afford to lose a few thousand homeless people or a bunch of trailers?"

"Hmm." I went to the section where the new books are shelved, hoping we'd had enough conversation to satisfy politeness.

Matthew followed me. "I recently donated a book that exposes the truth about the health care system." He ran his finger down the spines until he found the title *Pills and Other Lies*. "You're in luck. It's still here." Taking the book out, he shoved it toward me. "There's a really interesting chapter on fluoride treatments, which are full of industrial waste. The Russians put it in our water supply in order to lower the intelligence of the average American."

It certainly worked in your case. Instead of saying that aloud, I used Johnny Carson's old line. "I did not know that." Turning back to the shelf, I left him holding the book like a tray of hors d'oeuvres.

"There's also a chapter on the CIA's labs." Matthew is nothing if not determined. "That's where they create diseases like AIDS and

Ebola. Very useful for getting rid of certain elements, if you know what I mean."

Closing my eyes, I struggled to keep from answering. I tend to think there must be a way to present an argument so logically that the other person has to grant that it's true, but with a fanatic, it never, ever works.

It certainly wouldn't work with Matthew, who stood there with his book, obviously irritated that I wouldn't take it. "It's very well-written."

I picked out a paperback called *The Monk's Murder*. "I'm in the mood for a mystery, I think."

His lips pursed at the idea that a person would read fiction over the "facts" he offered. As I turned to go he said, "I'm sure you've heard we've got a criminal cruising the park."

Much as I hate letting Matthew have any sort of satisfaction, I was interested. "Criminal?"

"People see him moving between trailers, often late at night."

"I'm sure you told George."

"I did." Matthew's lips tightened again. "Not that he listens to what *I* say. But when he heard it from other people too, he had to take it seriously. The guy's a real bruiser." Matthew does this weird repeat of part of what he's just said. "Take it seriously."

"Good for George." I turned to go.

"Sure you don't want to try this book?" he asked, holding it out again.

"I'm sure." This time I quoted Belle from *Beauty and the Beast,* certain that Matthew, like Gaston, would miss the sarcasm. "But thanks for asking."

Chapter Nineteen

Ron (Ron & Julie) Friday 2:00 p.m.

I was outside wiping the pollen off my car when our neighbor, Isabel Schultz, came out of her trailer and approached her husband Harry, who was on his knees, manicuring the edge of his lawn with a pair of hand clippers. Isabel had brought him something on a napkin and a glass that tinkled with ice. Harry stopped work to eat and drink, and they talked, apparently about his work. As Isabel followed him around the trailer, he showed her several places of interest. I wondered how much she cared about weeds and fire ants—most wives don't—but it was nice to see them talking. They'd had a rough patch for a couple of years due to Isabel's mental issues. Recently she'd been diagnosed and received treatment, and things seemed to be smoothing out.

When they came back to the front, they saw me and waved a greeting. "Nice day," I called out.

Harry came closer so he didn't have to shout. "Did that man find you last night?"

"What man is that?"

"Young guy, kinda skinny. I told him I'd seen you leave, and he said he'd come back later."

"We went to hear the music group at the hall. Who was he?"

"Didn't say. Friendly, though—about talked my arm off."

Isabel had followed Harry, and she said, "He was looking in

your windows."

Harry made a subtle negative gesture, signaling I shouldn't pay attention to what she'd said. Isabel is prone to delusions, and I never know what to say when she tells a story that doesn't sound right. She's getting better with the medication, but I decided she wasn't a hundred percent yet.

She saw the gesture and took offense. "You know they're saying there's a peeper in the park, Harry."

"That was just guys talking. Mostly Del, and you know how he is."

Isabel spoke to me. "He was in your yard, not knocking on the door or anything."

"Maybe the park hired him to do some tree-trimming." Harry's tone turned mildly critical. "Your palm there could use some work."

"Yeah," I agreed. "My new knee has kept me from keeping up with my lawn chores."

"He was on his tiptoes, looking in their window." Isabel's brow furrowed. "I saw him."

Though Harry looked uncomfortable, he didn't argue with her. Probably has to choose his battles.

"Thanks for the heads-up," I told them. "I'll find out what he wanted when he comes back."

Chapter Twenty

Tommy (Tommy & Alice) Friday, 3:00 p.m.

Investigating for the police had sounded interesting when we were all together and excited about the idea, but it turned out to be more difficult than I expected. I'd never done more than greet most of the men on my list, yet I was supposed to start a conversation that would reveal their place of residence on a specific date in 1967. There's an old saying: "In theory, theory and practice are the same. In practice, they are not."

My biggest problem was that I'm no actor. No matter how well I rehearsed my speech, I ended up sounding like a man desperate for conversation. For example: following one guy into the mail room, I pulled an envelope from my box and said, "Huh. A letter from Nashville, Tennessee." He smiled in that vague way that indicates polite non-interest, but I went on. "I lived there when I was in my twenties. I suppose it's changed a lot since then."

"We stopped on our way down a while back," the guy said. "Wife wanted to see Music City and all that."

"That the only time you've been there?"

He gave me a look. "Yeah. Why do you ask?"

"Like I said, I wonder how different it is from when I was there."

"Look it up on the internet." He closed his mailbox and pocketed the key. "You can find out anything there."

I got lucky a few times, finding men willing to talk about almost anything. One was ex-military and had been stationed in Germany from '65 to '70. After a session of pool volleyball, I struck up a conversation with a man from northern California who admitted he'd wandered the U.S. mainland through most of the sixties. "I was a vagabond hippie type back then," he said, "looking for Nirvana." He draped his towel around his neck, adding, "The perfect state of being, not the band."

"Do you remember them all? Like, where were you in the summer of 1967?"

His wife had joined us, still toweling herself dry. "Taos, right, Ronnie? We sold art the whole summer that year."

"Yeah," he agreed. "Commercial images were big at that time. We took stuff we saw in ads and turned it into art: t-shirts with dish scrubbers and soup cans on them. We called it new realism, but it ended up known as pop art."

"Oh, yeah, like Andy Warhol."

My comment made the woman's lips twist, and I guessed there was supposed to be more to pop art than one guy.

"We're big fans of Lichtenstein," the man said. When I looked confused he added, "He made those large paintings of comic strip scenes, emphasizing the small dots of color that blend in the small print of a newspaper page."

The wife added, "Geniuses like Lichtenstein and Warhol forced viewers to consider the fine line that exists between art and commercial design."

"Right. Did you ever visit Nashville?"

They both laughed at the idea. "What's in Nashville?" she

asked. “Country music and a bunch of hicks.” Belatedly realizing that might offend me she added, “I mean, some people like it, but we’re more Bob Dylan than Buck Owens.”

It went on like that. Sometimes I was able to eliminate a man; other times my reward was a vague, “I’m not sure.” My failures were mostly due to my inability to come up with realistic reasons for asking. “I should stick to reading mysteries instead of trying to solve them,” I told Alice. “I make a horrible detective.”

“It’s not your fault you’re a bad liar.” She gave my arm a little squeeze. “In all cases except this one, it’s the way a man should be.”

Chapter Twenty-One

Julie (Ron & Julie) Friday, 3:00 p.m.

I called Detective O'Connor Friday afternoon to tell him the sleuthing project was underway. Though I guessed he didn't spend much time thinking about us during his busy workday, he responded with cautious optimism. Once I'd delivered the update, I asked a question I'd been wondering about. "The letter Kelly Ames got telling her where Greg Miles was living. Can you tell me more about it?"

It was none of my business, but O'Connor was polite. I hoped that meant he trusted me a little.

"The woman who wrote the letter lives in the Villages now, but she was at your park visiting friends. They attended a corn-hole tournament, and she heard this voice in the crowd that sounded familiar. It took her a while, but eventually she recognized it as Greg Miles. She said it was exactly the same voice: timbre, cadence, even word emphasis. She tried to locate the speaker in the crowd, but her vision isn't good these days. Still, she's convinced it was him."

"Why did she write to Kelly Ames about it?"

"She didn't feel like she could go to the police with something as vague as, 'I heard a voice in a crowd that I think was this guy who killed two people a long time ago.'" O'Connor added his own theory. "I'd say that knowing a murderer was something neither woman ever forgot, and she wanted to share the information with someone who'd relate. She and Ames had stayed in touch over the years with Christmas cards and the occasional phone call, and she told the police that Ames always felt guilty that she'd been the person who brought Miles to the apartment building. She believed she should have been able to tell the guy was no good."

"She isn't the first person who got taken in by some creep."

"Not by a long shot. Anyway, the friend wrote to Ames, having no idea she was too sick at that point to care about old lovers."

When we ended the call, I spent a few seconds wondering what it had been like for Kelly Ames to learn the man she was in love with was capable of brutally killing two innocent people. What had caused Greg Miles to do what he did that night? Since he'd been operating under an assumed name, it might not have been the first time he'd committed a crime. Was he a serial rapist? A psychotic murderer? Both? I reaffirmed my vow that we'd find Miles and see that he paid for what he'd done.

That afternoon, Wilma, Alice, and I attended a tea at the clubhouse. We asked Karen to come along, but she doesn't have much interest in what she calls "girlie pastimes." It was silly, for sure, but fun too. They had one of those goofy fashion shows where terms are taken literally. The "box jacket" was made from boxes, and the "tea dress" had teabags pinned all over the skirt. The "house coat" had windows and doors, and the "double-breasted suit" had—well, that one's pretty obvious.

As we walked home, Alice started telling how Matthew Nowicki had mansplained one of his conspiracy theories to her. Wilma stopped her to ask what mansplaining was. "It's when men tell women things in a patronizing way, assuming they're too dumb to have noticed or figured them out," Alice said, "like a guy at the office telling a female coworker how tough it is to move up the corporate ladder."

"I see," Wilma said, nodding. "Like when you go to buy a shear pin and the salesman tells you to be careful not to feed too much hay in at once, like you haven't baled hay your whole life."

Alice gave me a look, but I didn't have a clue what a shear pin was either, and I shrugged. "Yeah, like that," she said. "Tommy isn't really a man-splainer, but he does love explaining things. Last night he told me in great detail how Florida's weather works, that having the gulf on one side and the ocean on the other makes it hard to predict, yada, yada, yada. Like I don't watch the same weather channel he does."

"Ron's always lecturing me about how much electricity costs," I put in, "like I'm not the one who pays the bill every month."

Wilma never criticizes Earl, so I was shocked when she added her two cents. "The way Earl talks, you'd think I'm made of alabaster. 'Don't go outside, Wilma. There's a twenty percent chance of rain.'" She fiddled with the button on her sweater. "That murder last month made him even worse. You'd think I'm going to be sliced up into little pieces by some maniac if he's not right beside me to stop it from happening." She added something I wasn't sure she meant to say out loud. "What if we're not right for each other anymore?"

The question was followed by a moment of silence. I had no desire to jump into someone's marital difficulties and offer a solution, but Alice, braver and more outspoken than most, answered in a matter-of-fact tone. "Males often want more closeness with their partner as they age. Females tend to become more independent. For couples who've been together a long time, that's a hard change to deal with."

"Most of the time we do okay," Wilma said. "It's been kind of fun working together on our lists, and I don't mind watching shuffleboard that much. But when Earl talks about how it's his duty to keep me safe from absolutely everything, I feel like I'm not…like he thinks I couldn't survive without him."

"Well, you can," Alice said firmly. "Any one of us could make it alone if she had to."

Though Alice was the only one of us with experience at that, I think about it sometimes. On average, women live longer than men, and at a certain age we start mentally preparing to be alone. I think about what sort of widow I'd be, a social butterfly or a stay-at-home type. I mentally list the things I'd have no idea how to do without Ron. I consider what it must be like to have no one in the house to talk to, to laugh with, or even to argue with.

It's a horrible exercise, but I think we all do it.

Living at B-Bird is a constant reminder, since there are plenty of widows here. They help with events. They work on service projects. They "do lunch" together. Being alone can't be easy, but I admire that they take what life deals out and make the best of it.

Wilma's thoughts seemed to parallel mine. "I don't think I'd like being single."

"Don't dwell on it," Alice advised. "But recognize that if and when the time comes, you'll be okay."

Chapter Twenty-Two

Alice (Tommy & Alice) Friday p.m.

When we left the fashion show, Julie went to Wilma's to help her with where the punctuation would go on some needlepoint samplers she was making. As I went on alone, I passed #1 Gull Street and saw Terry Bidwell outside his place. Of course his wife Lila was close by. The Bidwells spend a lot of time working on their trailer. Terry was doing something to one of the awnings, and Lila was making herself useful, fetching tools he asked for and holding things that needed holding.

The couple is always together. In fact, I sometimes wonder if Terry gets to go into the bathroom by himself. Any conversation I had with him would include her, and I had to accept that.

"Good morning," I said, and they turned.

"Hello…" I read the thoughts that passed through Lila's head. *Look at the visitor. Think about who she is. Recall she's Tommy Murgasson's new wife. Come up with her name. Not Ella. That was the other one*. She smiled as it came to her. "Alice."

Terry let her handle the niceties as he went on removing set screws.

"How old is your trailer, do you know?"

Lila turned to Terry, who said, "Nineteen eighty-six."

"That's about the same as ours. Lots of upkeep."

"You got that right."

"When I was first married, we had one built in the fifties. At least these aren't quite as cramped as that one was."

Lila said, "That sounds uncomfortable." Terry said nothing

I soldiered on. "Things were different for wives back then. I think I spent eighty percent of my time in that trailer."

"I liked staying home," Lila said. "Being with the kids, taking care of the house, and having dinner for Terry when he came home." Her lips twitched. "Women would be better off today if they'd kept doing that instead of getting all liberated. What more important job is there than making a home and raising your kids?"

"That's exactly what I did." I didn't add that it had been because my first husband was a violent control freak.

Lila smiled. "Me too." Her tone turned rueful. "It makes it hard now, since I get no pension, but we did what was best for our family."

"Where are you from again?"

"Kennett, Missouri. It's almost to the Tennessee border." Lila went back to the subject of being a homemaker. "I made almost all the kids' clothes. I canned everything from beans to fish. I kept a few chickens for eggs and we burned wood we cut on our own property. Since Terry was gone a lot, I learned how to split it and everything."

"Where was he gone to?" I asked, but Lila appeared not to hear.

"I used to make pies for a local restaurant, which paid pretty good. Everyone loved my pies. Sometimes I did wedding cakes for people."

"You're a regular dynamo," I told her. "Now Terry, where were—"

"I sewed too, mostly alterations and repair, but sometimes more. I once did a whole wedding: bride's dress, bridesmaids, flower girl, and mother of the bride." She grinned. "I was one tired puppy by the time that was over."

"And what were—"

My attempt to turn the conversation to Terry went unheard. "I bet you won't believe this, but I even did work for the local funeral home. When they couldn't get anybody to fix the hair and do the makeup, I did it." Lila's face pinched. "I didn't like it, but I earned enough to get nice Christmas gifts for the kids that year."

Terry was focused on his awning repair, and his wife seemed determined to recall every cash job she'd ever had. I decided I'd have to try again later. As I started to walk away Terry said, "When a guy's on the road, traveling all over the place, it's good to know his wife is home taking care of everything."

Chapter Twenty-Three

Al (Al & Karen) Friday, 6:00 p.m.

You hear a lot about the stages of life, and there's no denying that we change over time. I used to be pretty strong; now I'm not. I used to have opinions about what's right and wrong in the world. Now I don't much care what goes on outside B-Bird Park. At thirty, or even at fifty, I couldn't have imagined how hard it would be to keep going at seventy-three, how getting dressed in the morning could wear me out and how taking a shower would mean I had to rest for a while afterward.

Still, the hunt for Greg Miles gave me a little boost of energy, and I stayed on my porch most of Friday, ready to do my part to find a killer. Willie Darner came by late in the afternoon, when the day is at its warmest and a lot of residents pour a glass of wine or a beer and sit on their patio. Willie's kind of a loner, but he's friendly enough if you speak first. When he came within hailing distance I asked if he wanted a beer. (I always ask. He always says no thanks.) Still, it appeared he had something on his mind that he wanted to share. Climbing the steps, he sat down opposite me.

"Do you think your buddy Tommy would go with me to see George at the office tomorrow morning? He's got more pull around this place than I do, but I'd sure like to see some changes made."

"Like what?"

"More security, for one thing. We should have somebody locking up the buildings every night and opening them up in the morning."

"Who's going to do that?"

"They could hire someone, or maybe one of us could do it for a little cut off our rent. You know we got strangers hanging around the park, and it irritates me no end when I see outsiders dump their garbage in our trash bins or help themselves to the stuff in the Free Store. If we should lock everything up at night, maybe they'll go someplace else."

"I don't know, Willie. Residents like the convenience of being able to get in where they want to any time of the day."

"But what about this guy we got wandering the park at night? Do they want him getting in wherever he wants?" Willie's completely bald, and the muscles in his head twitch when he's riled up about something. "I bet he's homeless and living for free in the park." Pointing vaguely as he spoke, he went on, "We got showers and toilets in the clubhouse. There's a nice, soft rug he can sleep on in the library. And I'll bet he sneaks into the hall when nobody's looking, hides in a closet, then raids the refrigerator after everybody goes home."

"You've thought this through."

"If I was homeless, it's what I'd do. People around here are patsies, and George is as bad as the rest. When I tried to tell him this guy's probably living in our buildings, he laughed. He doesn't even care that we could have a serial killer wandering our streets."

"Talk to Tommy," I advised, though I realized I was passing the buck. "He'll go with you to talk to George."

Willie leaned his forearms on his thighs. "People don't want to think about how dangerous the world is, you know? They want to pretend everything is fine…right up to the time when it isn't. Then they say, 'Why didn't somebody warn us about this?'" After a pause he repeated, "People are patsies."

It was time to change the subject. "I watched that movie *The Dirty Dozen* for about the tenth time yesterday. Do you remember that one?"

"Sure," Willie responded. "It's a classic." He wasn't quite over his anger with the modern world, and he added, "Back then people knew how to take care of business. Lee Marvin wasn't no patsy."

"I saw it when it first came out in '67," I said, ignoring the actor's macho-ness. "Did you see it then?"

His head wrinkled again. "Yeah, I think so."

"I was in Pittsburg that summer." I said that like I hadn't been a resident of Pittsburgh my whole life. "Where'd you live back then?"

Screwing up his face, Willie searched his brain for the answer. "In '67? I was in Denver. Why?"

"No reason. What were you doing there?"

Willie grinned. "Being a ski bum. I was convinced I'd be the next Jean-Claude Killy." He smiled at the dreams of his younger self.

"What does a ski bum do besides ski? I mean, to earn money?"

"We were real Peter Pan types. We only cared about the sport, so we avoided growing up for as long as we could." Willie clasped his hands and laid them on his belly as he reminisced. "I stayed in this horrible apartment with five other guys. Lots of times we took jobs that paid in pizza, or we worked in those tourist hotels where your ID badge has your hometown listed under your name. It was all okay with us as long as we got as many days on the mountain as possible."

"Sounds like a crazy way to live."

"My personal record was having four jobs at once. I had a 25-year old classic Oldsmobile that had a heater that worked maybe one day a week. It had multi-colored body parts, and we loaded it down with stickers to hide the rust." Willie shook his head. "I was still better off than a lot of my friends that had to travel by bike no matter what the weather. They'd attach their skis to the bike frames with PVC tubing."

"And did all those indignities ever pay off?"

He sniffed. "I never made it to nationals, much less the Olympics."

Willie's wistful tone convinced me he was telling the truth, but I gave it one more shot. "I thought somebody said you lived in Nashville back in the day."

"You mean Nashville, Tennessee? Nope. I never came east of the Mississippi until Shirley and I met online a few years ago. When we hit it off, we both sold our houses and moved down here." He grinned. "Those computer dating sites are convenient, but they sure mess up a guy's geography."

When Willie went on his way, and I sat there feeling fake, even cheesy, for tricking him into talking about his past. We'd been eager to start the project, and we hadn't thought it through very well. Our methods were diverse, our results spotty, and we had more question marks than certainties. Of the eight of us, only Earl and Wilma claimed to be certain that everyone they'd talked to was completely okay.

Chapter Twenty-Four

Tommy (Tommy & Alice) Friday-Saturday

On Friday, we met after dinner to begin whittling down the master list. Each of us had been able to eliminate some interviewees, or at least put them into the unlikely category. Ron reported that a man on Egret Street with a pronounced limp had contracted polio as a child. "It's possible he's lying," he told us, "but he talked about missing second grade and having to watch his friends play ball from a bench on the sidelines. His story seems legit."

I wondered how he'd explored that painful subject when I was having trouble even getting a conversation started in most cases.

Al commented that our roundabout approaches made it hard to get specifics. When several others agreed, Julie chewed at her bottom lip and insisted, "We'll get better as we go."

Earl and Wilma were moving so quickly through their lists that I wondered how thorough they'd been. Wilma seemed convinced that anyone who attended church couldn't possibly be our man, and Earl has a tendency to believe that people don't lie, simply because he doesn't. That might lead them to dismiss candidates prematurely. I wondered if I should have a private word with Julie and suggest that some of us re-check the people Earl and Wilma claimed they'd proven innocent.

Despite my doubts, I had to face the fact that everyone in the group was ahead of me. I was hopelessly inept at asking intrusive questions, especially to strangers.

Julie had spoken with O'Connor again, and she relayed a few

more details on the murders. As I listened, a question came to mind. “You said this guy was already using an alias when he came to Nashville. How did he manage that?”

“He stole a wallet from a coma patient at a care facility. The police found the real Greg Miles in Arizona.”

As usual, Alice saw where I was going. “Then this man was a criminal before he came to Nashville and killed those people.”

“I assume the police looked at people who worked at the nursing home,” I said.

Julie nodded. “The staff and the patient’s relatives all checked out.”

I considered that. “A search for a local man who went missing at that time might bring better results now that records are digitized.”

“But it won’t do us any good.” Al tapped his list with a finger. “The guy who stole Greg Miles’ identity back then has been using some other name for over fifty years.”

“That’s true, but there might be a photo, or fingerprints on file.”

Karen chuckled. “Next you’ll want a sample of each man’s prints.”

“That’s up to the police. All we can do is keep at our lists.” Ron rubbed the back of his neck. “I had one guy tell me to mind my own business though. Not sure how to go forward with him.”

“How about we switch names if we contact someone and get nowhere?” Al suggested. “It won’t be so obvious if a new person talks to ’em.”

“Good idea,” Alice said. “A different approach might get results.”

We spent a few minutes rearranging our lists, which the ever-efficient Julie promised would result in new ones by tomorrow. You can't keep a good librarian down, even in retirement.

When the meeting broke up, I still had reservations. If two different people started a conversation and brought up the same date, our subjects might well wonder what was up. Since I didn't have a better idea, I went along.

That evening, I discovered I'd made a mistake earlier in the day that was likely to set my marriage back about a century. For Alice and me, the first year of marriage had been rocky. The woman I'd known casually for three months and dated for three more, a person who was funny and smart and easy to talk to, turned angry only a few weeks after we made our vows. Alice criticized me, at home and in public, lashing out when I least expected it. For months I walked on eggshells, trying to avoid her anger and usually failing miserably.

We had a breakthrough in December, when I made a mistake that forced us to talk about our relationship. We learned what most people do when honest discussion replaces carping and silent resentment: We had each misunderstood the other's intentions. Alice lacks confidence in herself and in the institution of marriage. Her way of coping was to try to control everything I did, said, and thought. The fact that she didn't care who knew when she was angry didn't help the situation.

It was a revelation to me that my Texas manners increased my wife's insecurity. I was raised to believe that courteous men tell women how attractive they are, eloquently and often. Alice saw my compliments to other women as belittling to her. In the end we agreed I'd tone down the Texas charm and she'd try to be more trusting. That was all good.

Despite our recent progress, a guy sometimes wanders back into trouble, despite the best of intentions.

With my first wife, Ella, I had three kids, now grown and well-established in life. Two of them had come to Florida with their families for winter break, and my older daughter called to suggest we join them for a day at Busch Gardens. Alice had been out when the call came, and I was so pleased with the invitation that I didn't think about waiting to ask if she was willing. Alice loves Busch Gardens, and we had no plans for the day. "Sure," I told Corinne. "We'll meet you at the entrance tomorrow around ten."

"What if I don't want to spend all day with your girls?" Alice said that night when I finally remembered to tell her.

Hearing a tone that reminded me of the recent, unhappy past, I tried to be positive. "It'll be fun. We'll eat too much, watch the critters, and then come home."

"They don't like me."

My girls do have reservations about my second marriage. Growing up in the household of Professor Murgasson and his proper wife Ella, they had views on people who spend a lot of time in bars. I'd met Alice when she poured beers at the 19th Hole, and she made no apologies for how she earned her living. Alice had escaped an abusive marriage with few choices, no financial support, and two boys to raise. I'd shared that with my slightly snooty daughters, but it didn't help. They'd looked down their noses at her from the start.

If Alice had been the sweet and silent type, my girls might have overcome their reservations, but life taught her that sweet and silent got a woman nowhere. The first time Alice called me out for a minor fault in front of the whole Murgasson clan, the girls looked at me, and then at each other, in horror. From then on, I heard disapproval in their voices whenever they spoke of Alice or to her.

It's hard to talk honestly with grown children about a new

spouse. I'm not sure the kids get how hard it is to start over in your seventh decade, getting used to a new person in your life. Alice and I love each other, but late in life, love is different from the hearts and flowers emotion of youth. It's about respecting each other and being willing to accept that we're all molded by the years—decades—that came before we met. I was wrong to agree to a family day without consulting Alice. Believe me, I did some fancy footwork to make up for it.

"Why would you say yes without at least checking with me, Tommy?" I cringed at the old shrillness that crept into Alice's voice. Ron was across the street, sitting at his patio table, but if he overheard, he gave no sign of it. He's my friend, so he wouldn't.

"We won't stay long, maybe three hours," I promised.

"Three hours should give those two all kinds of nasty things to say about me after I leave." Leaning against the kitchen counter, Alice folded her arms, her posture daring me to claim that wasn't true.

"I'll steer the talk away from any topics that set Corinne off." My eldest is politically opinionated and prone to lecture.

"Good luck with that," Alice sneered.

"And the grandkids like spending time with you."

"Despite their mothers' opinions."

"Alice, I'm sorry. I wanted to spend time with my family in an atmosphere where everyone's relaxed. I didn't think you'd mind, and I apologize for leaving you out of the decision."

She unfolded her arms. "They're your family, Tommy, and you deserve to see them when you can." After a moment she added, "But if I pinch your elbow at any point, immediately invent an excuse for us to leave."

Relieved, I promised, "Deal."

Chapter Twenty-Five

Wilma (Earl & Wilma) Saturday, 9:00 a.m.

One of the men on my contact list was Matthew Nowicki. Even though Earl and I had agreed to work together, I decided I'd do better alone on that interview. None of the men like Matthew very much, and things turned worse when he tattled on Tommy at Christmas time. Some mischief with lawn decorations. I never heard all the details.

Matthew can be a bit self-centered, but he's a staunch Christian and good about assisting at park events. I have to twist Earl's arm to get him to decorate the hall for a holiday or plant flowers along the walkways, but Matthew is always first in line when the call goes out for help. Alice says he has to make himself useful or he wouldn't have anybody to talk to, but she's still mad at him about the Christmas thing.

Anyway, I got my chance to talk to him while we removed and stored the last of the chapel's winter décor. Matthew was a gentleman, insisting that his wife Taffy and I stay on the ground while he climbed the ladder to reach the high stuff. He handed the items to Taffy, who brought them to me, and I put them into the boxes where they belong. I have them all clearly marked, so if I don't return some year, whoever has the job next will know what's available.

"It's time to start planning the Senior Prom," I said. "Will you two be there this year?"

"We wouldn't miss it," Taffy replied. "I love seeing everyone all dressed up and the guys with their numbers."

It is encouraged (but not required) that at our winter formal dance, couples make a sign the men wear on the backs of their suit jackets, telling how many years they've been married. Like a lot of things in senior communities, these signs have become a kind of contest to see who can make the most beautiful, innovative, or unique ones. Some are crocheted, some knitted, and some painted on canvas with palm trees and flamingoes in the background. Beaders make theirs with cloisonné or Swarovski crystals; cross-stitchers make colorful little *X*'s. Earl's is done in sequins on black velvet, so it sparkles in the lights overhead. I've already picked out the stitches from last year's *7* and chosen the colors to make an *8*.

"We're at forty-eight years," I told them. "How about you?"

"Forty-six." Pausing with an elbow on the stepladder, Matthew volunteered the information I wanted. "My parents were missionaries in the Philippines, and I grew up there. For me, high school was done by correspondence." He raised a finger. "Nobody went easy on me because I was overseas. In fact, I think the teachers were harder on me than they were on kids they saw every day. It's lucky I have a good mind and a strong work ethic." Clearing his throat he repeated, "Work ethic."

It's a little mental tic Matthew has, repeating part of what he says after he's said it. He also brags a little too much. And then there are things he believes, which Julie and Alice say are nuts, like we never really landed on the moon or the pyramids were built by aliens. I don't claim to know anything about it, but I have watched TV shows on both those topics. It's hard to say what's true and what isn't.

"Growing up in a strange country must have been hard." Though I was digging for more information, I did have trouble imagining life in a place where you never see a cornfield or a pine tree.

Matthew's chest puffed a little. "I'm very adaptable." As he went on, he returned to taking down garland. "By the time I finished high school, I knew I wanted to live in the good old U.S. of A. There's no place even close to it on this earth, in spite of all the shenanigans our government gets up to."

I hurried to encourage recall rather than a rant on how awful things were in Washington, D.C. "Did your family come home then?"

"Only me. My parents owned a house in Connecticut, and they let me live there."

"When was that?

"Oh, 1970, I think. I worked for a few years delivering goods, but then I got a job driving school bus. Taffy and I got married in '74." After a second he repeated, "Married in '74."

Matthew wasn't Greg Miles. I could officially mark him off my list.

"Well, you two make a really cute couple."

Matthew elbowed his wife. "Taffy knows a good thing when she's got it, right, Hon?"

Her eyes shone with affection. "You're the best, Matthew."

I picked up a box. "Well, let's get these things stored so you two can be on your way."

After Taffy and Matthew left, I heard someone out front and turned to see Del Hanna. "I was about to lock up," I told him, closing the storeroom door, "but if you need something…"

"I wondered if you'd like to practice our duet a little more."

"Oh. I thought we were coming along pretty well."

"Practice makes perfect." He spoke in a mock-chiding manner.

Had Del heard something in my singing that needed work? He was musically trained, while I'd picked up what I knew as I went along. Still, it felt weird to be there with only the two of us.

Then I remembered Del was on my list of men to contact. "All right. Let's run through it." As he got the music out and sat down at the piano I started the story we'd concocted. "Earl and I started dating in 1967," I said. "We were talking last night about how different it was back then."

"Yes." He sounded distracted as he paged through the book for the right song.

"Where were you that summer?"

"Huh?"

"In 1967. Where were you?"

"Springfield, Ohio." Finding the page, he set the book on the music rack. "There we go."

"What did you do for a living in Springfield?"

"I told you. I had a band," Del answered.

"Did you travel? Go to places like Toledo or…Nashville?"

"For a while. Being on the road gets old fast, though."

"When exactly did your band travel?"

He turned to me. "From the late '60s to '71. Why?"

My palms had grown damp. "No reason. It must have been exciting, visiting lots of places and meeting all sorts of people."

"Most of the time it was a lot of work. The other guys in the band all had day jobs, so I drove the truck to wherever we had a gig and unloaded the equipment. By the time they got to the club or whatever, I'd have everything all set up."

"So you drove the truck, and you traveled alone."

"Mostly." Del shifted his shoulders. "Now let's see if we can do this a cappella before we try it with the piano."

When we'd done that, I said I had to go. Del stepped ahead of me and opened the door, wearing a look that made me feel like Little Red Riding Hood on her way into the forest. "Let's meet before practice on Wednesday and work on it again."

"I don't—"

"Wilma." Del looked at me from under his brows. "Do I make you nervous?"

"No, of course not."

"Because I'm not the kind of man who'd ever take advantage of a woman." His teeth flashed. "Even one as attractive as you."

"Right. Earl will be waiting for his lunch." It was a lame excuse, since it was only mid-morning, but it was all I could manage.

Del showed no sign of disappointment. "Let's say a half hour before practice on Wednesday."

"Twenty minutes." I sidled toward the door. "It's only a few lines."

As I passed him in the aisle, Del squeezed my arm. "I'll see you then."

Chapter Twenty-Six

Karen (Al & Karen) Saturday a.m.

It was interesting to watch each person in our little group go at the task we'd set for ourselves, like Ron and his slot-car idea, and Al with some World War II movie. I tried to approach each target at a neutral place, in the laundry room or during the informal street gatherings that happen daily around the park. I'd start a conversation and then steer it toward what Springsteen calls "Glory Days." It was kind of interesting, and I learned a lot about men I barely knew. Some had been in the military that year, some in college, and some settled in with a wife and a kid or two. As soon as I was able to, I zeroed in on July 7th, saying Al and I had visited a cousin of his in Nashville and the date stuck with me because of a double murder that happened nearby.

Nobody batted an eye. Not one guy shifted his feet or put up a hand to cover his mouth, which I understand is a sign a person is lying. I got nothing but polite interest.

Because it was dependent on "accidental" meetings and trips down Memory Lane, my method was slow. Out of my first three tries, one response was specific enough for me to rule the guy out—again, if he'd told the truth and if my powers of discernment were correct.

Julie's approach was more direct. She told the men on her list that she and Ron had had an argument about whether couples meet by fate or by accident. To prove her contention that it was fate, she'd chosen a number of men at random from the park directory, intending to find out where they were on the night she and Ron first met.

I didn't find that particularly believable, but Julie contends she's done stranger things to prove a point. "When Ron and I disagreed on how much our son should charge for lawn work, I spent two weeks asking everyone who came into the library what a minor child should get paid for an hour of mowing. I added the numbers up and took an average, and it came out a whole lot closer to my figure than Ron's." Picking up her list, she got back to business. "Guys laugh about this fate thing, but not one has refused to answer, at least not outright."

"What does that mean?"

"One guy claimed he couldn't remember, and another said he was somewhere in the Mid-Atlantic States. He was a surveyor's apprentice, so they moved every few days."

"Then those two need to be re-interviewed by someone else."

She sighed. "I hope it doesn't become too obvious that we're all asking about one date and one place. You know how everything that happens at B-Bird gets commented on."

"And analyzed and questioned. We aren't going to get away with our little stories for long."

"They can speculate all they want. In a week or so, we'll be done and there'll be new gossip to discuss." She put down her pen. "I like my story, and I'm refining it as I go so it gets more believable each time."

I let it go at that. When it comes to skullduggery, to each her own.

Chapter Twenty-Seven

Tommy (Tommy and Alice) Saturday, 12:10 p.m.

Our day at Busch Gardens went pretty well at first. The grandkids are teenagers and therefore unlikely to admit they're enjoying anything, but they couldn't hide their interest in the giraffes, rhinos, and other exotic animals. My sons-in-law were great, taking positions at the back of the group like cowboys riding drag, pushing their progeny along while the kids used their cell phones to give minute-to-minute updates to their friends. Corinne and Carol chatted with Alice and me, asking about life at B-Bird as if it were the most interesting topic imaginable.

That lasted until lunch. Over tacos and enchiladas Corinne asked, "Did you see what the Secretary of Education proposed last week, Dad? Parent oversight of school behavior codes." A high school math teacher, Corinne also serves as education association president. To Alice she said, "You can't imagine how irritating it is for those of us who work in the schools to have amateurs interfere with policy."

The comment was insulting on two levels: the assumption that parents should remain out of school affairs, and the hint that Alice was too ignorant to grasp the problems of academia.

"I'm sure it's frustrating for you." Alice's overly sweet tone should have served as a warning. "As a parent I always supported my sons' teachers unless they gave me reason not to."

"Well, of course you did. The teacher is a professional—"

"—Hired to do what's best for kids," Alice interrupted. "Of

course, parents should get input as to what that is."

Corinne made a visible effort not to sputter. "Surely you're not saying that teachers have to—"

"Look at that elephant!" I pointed, though all that was visible from our table was a large, gray ear. "I bet the kids will want a picture with her later. Eat up, kids. Gotta move on."

Later Davy, my second-oldest grandson, mentioned he planned to spend the gift card we'd sent him for Christmas on something called Splatoon. His mother had to put in her two cents' worth. "The boys like the gift cards, Alice," Carol said. "Mother always got each grandchild a present that was personal, but I think you're wise not to try that."

"A smart step-grandma never tries to replace the original one," Alice replied. "Even if the real grandma is gone forever."

Spinning like a dervish, I turned to address the group and cut off any possible reply Carol might make. "Wasn't that elephant something? Probably the biggest elephant I've ever seen. Davey, did you get some good pictures?"

As we drove home, I waited for the explosion of resentment Alice was no doubt holding in. Instead she said, "That was a nice time, don't you think? I enjoyed myself, and I think the kids did too."

I was pleased to hear it, and of course I didn't tell her that when she hugged me goodbye, Carol had whispered that I was welcome to come home to Montana anytime and live with her and Raymond.

Chapter Twenty-Eight

Julie (Ron & Julie) Saturday, 12:30 p.m.

The excuse I invented for my interviews worked like a dream until it turned into a nightmare. I didn't get iron-clad proof of anyone's guilt or innocence, but I had the sense the men I'd talked to were okay. They answered my question. They chuckled. If they were a little patronizing about my going to such lengths to prove my husband wrong, that was okay with me.

Then I approached Ty Shaw. Spotting him in the food line at the kielbasa luncheon, helping himself to sauerkraut and beans, I hurried to the end of the line. Once he had his hands full with his plate and his beverage cup, I offered to carry his dessert of choice to his table. On the way, I asked my question. Ty's wife Nan, who'd skipped the dessert table entirely, came up behind us and overheard my story, and before I knew it, I wasn't in control of the situation any more. Struck with the idea of where Fate puts us at any given time, Nan had one of her big ideas. When that happens, she's unstoppable, like a high school cheerleader with a plan for the next pep rally.

"What a great way to bring people together," Nan said, clasping her hands. "You should get everybody in the park to tell where they were on that date. We could make a big map that shows all the locations. I bet we'd find out that some of us were connected long before we ended up here." She stopped to think. "What day were you asking about?"

"Um, July 7, 1967."

"Huh." Her pretty face scrunched for a second. "There are better choices, like the moon landing or JFK's assassination, but we can work with that one, since you already started. We'll call it 'Park Crossings.'" Her gesture suggested a banner that covered a wide swathe of space.

My heart sank. Knowing Nan well, I realized that "we" was actually me. Nan sees herself as an "idea person." Others are expected to turn her suggestions into reality, at which point she steps in to share the credit.

The sparkle in Nan's eyes said she was already envisioning the completed project. "People will love it."

I stood there with my mouth open. Without saying a word, much less the word *yes*, my excuse for talking to less than twenty men had turned into a park-wide undertaking, with Nan as cheerleader and me as drudge.

She wasn't wrong. The finished product was sure to be popular, since we love discovering connections within our group of apparent strangers. You talk to someone from Ohio and learn you went to school with his nephew. You mention your hometown, and someone says they used to vacation near there. Once Tommy mentioned a classic car he used to own, and one of the men in the group had bought that same car from the person Tommy sold it to. We're hundreds of miles from home, yet we keep finding little hooks to each other in our past.

The problem was that I didn't want to interview everyone in the park. I tried to worm my way out of it. "I've got a busy few weeks coming up, Nan. Lots of…letters to write."

She waved a hand. "I can get you a ton of volunteers. B-Birders are always looking for interesting things to do." Putting a hand on my arm she ordered, "You come up with a plan, tell us what you need done, and we'll get it done."

The idea of posting everyone's whereabouts on a random date fifty-plus years ago apparently appealed to a lot of people. Volunteers began showing up at our door that very afternoon, and I was also approached in the library, in the mailroom, and as Ron and I walked that evening. "I can cover my whole street," Glenda from Brooklyn offered, and Carrie Burns chimed in, "I'll do Gull Street, no problem."

But there was a problem. I had specific suspects to interview. I needed to see their reactions when they were asked about the date. I told them, as I'd told everyone else, "I'll get back to you."

Glenda and Carrie went off, their heads inclined toward each other as they no doubt wondered aloud why I hadn't thanked them all over the place. Alice and Tommy had spent the day at Busch Gardens, but when I told her what had happened, she laughed in delight. "Your mistake was making it sound like fun, Julie. Ask for help weeding the picnic area, and they'll run the other way."

"I think I'm really going to have to do this," I said ruefully. "Who'd have guessed everyone would get so excited about a chart?"

"'No good deed goes unpunished.'" Alice nudged me with an elbow. "Next time you talk to O'Connor, tell him you're going to need compensation for poster board and push pins."

I suspected Ron found my predicament funny too, though he was careful not to say it aloud. While I got the humor at least a little, it wasn't easy to come up with a way to refuse help I didn't want and still complete the work I'd started.

Things got worse Saturday evening, when there came a knock at my door. Peeking out the window to see who it was, I let out a little moan. Known as a tireless worker, Jessica LaTran is also a difficult person to deal with. She has her own ideas about everything, and she doesn't take no for an answer. Jessica (never Jessie or Jess) is statuesque, with small, ice-blue eyes that seem to bore right into your soul. I get nervous when I talk to her, even if it's a completely innocuous conversation. Under that gaze I feel like every word I say is being weighed and applied to a list of my faults. With a sigh, I went out to greet her.

"I heard about this display thing you plan to make," she said, waving a hand to indicate she didn't need to come inside. "I'm willing to do all the interviews." I opened my mouth to give a firm "No, thank you," but she went right on. "You're going to be busy collating the information and making the chart. I figure if I visit thirty trailers a day, it will take me a week and a half to get the job done. I'll bring my results by every evening, so you can enter the data in small batches."

"That's nice of you, Jessica, but several others have volunteered to help. It will be faster—"

She made a dismissive sound. "You can't let just anybody do this, Julie. Some will do a little bit and then lose interest." She made a final, unrelenting statement. "You need one responsible person who'll do it right and stay on it till the job's done."

"That's nice of you but—"

"I was thinking you could go to that printing place in Spring Hill and have them make a large map of the U.S. When I give you the locations each day, you can put a pushpin in and connect it to the name of the resident with yarn."

"It's more than the U.S. We've got the Canadians, and people who were overseas back then, soldiers and nurses in Vietnam, Peace Corps workers, and missionaries. We need the whole world."

She nodded. "Okay, get a world map."

"But it would have to be huge to fit all the U.S. residents in."

"Huh," she said, frowning. "It will definitely have to be big." Leaning toward me like a stern teacher, she asked, "Where are you going to put the display?"

"In the meeting hall, Nan says, on the long wall."

"Best place for everyone to see it." She shifted her feet. "I'll start tomorrow morning on the interviews."

"Let me get back to you on that. As I mentioned, others—"

"And as I told you, I prefer to do it all myself," she interrupted. "That way the results will be standardized."

"Look, I appreciate the offer, but I'm the one who has to figure out how this will be done. A lot of people want to help, and since the whole park is involved, I'm not willing to tell them no." Her face turned stony, and I tried to ignore it as I finished, "I'll contact you as soon as I have a plan." I had to raise my voice at the last, because Jessica was already stalking away like an offended ostrich.

Chapter Twenty-Nine

Ron (Ron & Julie) Saturday, 3:00 p.m.

One of the nice things about living in a community like B-Bird is that you can borrow almost anything you need. Since Saturday afternoon was cool and we'd finished off the last of the oatmeal cookies, Julie was struck with the urge to make an angel food cake. She doesn't have one of those weird pans with the removable bottom and the cone in the middle here in Florida, but all it took was a request on the park's Facebook page. Within an hour I was on my way to # 16 Bittern Street to get a loaner.

The guy who answered the door looked confused when I told him what I'd come for. His wife had gone somewhere and failed to mention I'd be stopping by. "Angel food cake pan, huh?" He opened a series of cabinets in the kitchen, revealing every kind of baking pan, tool, and device known to man, though in this case it would be known to woman. This man didn't know an angel food cake pan from a soup pot.

"I think that's it right there." I pointed, and he got the two pieces out, frowned at them in consternation, and handed them to me. "Thanks. We'll get it back to you by tomorrow afternoon."

"Fine by me." He started closing all the doors he'd opened. "My wife has plenty of other choices for baking, as you can see."

"It's a wonder you don't weigh three hundred pounds."

He chuckled and cupped his rounded belly. "I'm not getting any skinnier. Luckily, Dethel gives away a lot of what she makes. There's always a bazaar in the works, and there's my cousin Taffy, who doesn't even know how to turn on her oven. Dethel sees that she and Matthew get half a cake or a dozen cookies every few days."

"You're Taffy Nowicki's cousin?"

"We're the reason they came to B-Bird. They visited us, liked the place, and decided to buy here."

That wasn't a red-letter day for the park in my opinion, but I kept my comment tactful. "Taffy seems like a sweet person."

"She is." A bit defensively he added, "Matthew can be kind of a pain, but he's not bad once you get past the bragging and that 'everybody's out to get you' stuff."

"I have wondered why he's so convinced there's a plot around every corner."

"His parents were kind of weird. They took him overseas when he was about two, and they preached a lot about how evil the world is. So he was isolated with two very paranoid people. It's bound to make a kid scared." The guy shrugged. "I think Matthew dealt with his fears by convincing himself he's smarter than everyone else. Only he sees what's 'real.' Only he understands how messed up society is." He chuckled. "That's my five cents' worth of amateur psychology."

Seeing a chance to check the information Wilma had submitted on Matthew, I said, "I suppose you know him pretty well. You've been around him for about fifty years, right?"

He did a quick calculation. "Fifty-three. We met in 1967, right after I graduated from Middletown High." He glanced at a photo on the wall that showed a smiling young couple in bell-bottom jeans. "Taffy had been talking about this guy from the Philippines for a while, and one day she brought him over to our table at the A&W." He grinned. "Next thing I knew, he was telling me he was on the

CIA's watch list because he was an outspoken critic of Lyndon Johnson. I was pretty sure from the get-go that neither the CIA nor LBJ had ever heard of Matthew Nowicki." Clearing his throat, the man shifted gears. "But he isn't a bad person if you ignore all the goofy stuff."

I know better than to criticize a person's relatives, even if he starts it. "We all want to leave our mark on the world."

Belatedly, he held out his hand. "I'm Garrett Pennell, by the way. I've seen you around, but I don't think we're ever been introduced."

"Ron Rogers, and I'd better get this pan to my wife or I won't get any dessert after dinner."

Back home, I told Julie about the conversation while she mixed up the cake batter. When I mentioned the year, she stopped working. "He said they met in '67?"

"I knew that would interest you."

She went to her tablet and did some checking. "Wilma's notes say Matthew was in the Philippines until 1970."

"It's something we should nail down."

"Yes." Julie's whole body sagged. "How many others either lie about their past or remember it wrong?" She returned to the cake, mixing harder as her anxiety level rose. "Detective O'Connor trusted us to get this done, and now we can't be sure our data is correct. And Nan's got this big idea going, and everybody has an opinion on how that should be done." Her voice wavered a little. "Stuff is raining on my head too fast. I can't organize it into workable segments."

"Hey, we'll get it done," I assured her. "And we aren't

responsible for who lies or gets his answer mixed up. We do what O'Connor asked. After that, he'll take the ball and run with it."

"You're right, but you know I hate doing a job halfway."

After five decades with her, I knew both the good and the bad sides of Julie's zeal for whatever her current project was. Nothing less than a hundred percent will do for her, and too often she gets upset over things nobody can control. "All we can do is what we promised, Babe."

"Yes." Her voice firmed again. "I'll make really good notes, and I'll star names we think they should look at more closely."

"We'll eliminate the easy ones. O'Connor has the tools to take it from there."

"You always know how to make me feel better," she said. "Which means you deserve a treat." She poured the batter into the pan and used a spatula to clear the sides. Tipping it up so it didn't drip, she handed the batter-coated utensil to me.

There are things a person never outgrows, and for me, licking the spoon is high on that list.

Chapter Thirty

Karen (Al & Karen) Sunday, 9:00 a.m.

When I stopped at Julie's Sunday morning, she sat at the computer desk on the lanai, chin in one hand. "Hey, kid, what's happening?"

She motioned me in and pointed to the couch, inviting me to sit. "You know my idea, the argument Ron and I were supposedly having about how two people meet? Well, Nan Shaw heard about it, and she thinks 'we'—meaning me—should find out where every single person in the park was on that date."

"Why?"

She sighed. "She wants me to make a big display to show how the residents came from all over and ended up here. 'Building community,' she calls it."

"Well, tell her you don't want to."

Julie chuckled. "You have met Nan, right? Two seconds after the idea hit her, she was telling everyone around us what a cool thing I was going to do and how great it will be when everyone gets to see the results. She's talking about having some sort of party for the unveiling. How could I admit I only meant to contact seventeen men?"

"Simple. You say, 'Nan, I don't want to do that."

"She was so excited, Karen, and I hate disappointing…" With a rueful grin, Julie stopped herself.

"You hate disappointing anyone, so you do things you really don't want to do to make them happy. You are too nice, Julie Rogers."

That brought a snort of anger, but it was directed at herself. "I'm not nice. I'm...spineless. I'm weak. I'm a pushover." Picking up a sheet of paper with drawings all over it, she said, "I'm working on how it can be done, but it will take hours and hours of canvassing and collating. Plus, Nan's picturing the display as something fancy, and I'm no artist." She chuckled grimly. "The instructor at art class tries so hard to find something to praise in my paintings. 'That's really colorful,' she'll say, or, 'You're good with shapes.' What she means is my trees look like green triangles and everything else is out-of-whack rectangles."

"Get Wilma to help," I suggested. "She's creative, and she has all kinds of crafty odds and ends."

Julie's face brightened. "That's a great idea." But she wasn't done listing problems. "Even if she can make it pretty, I don't know how I'll fit hundreds of bits of information onto one chart."

I scratched at my neck. "Could you use a template, like the ones they have for address labels? Alice would probably help you type the information in, and then you could print the labels and stick them where you want them on a big map."

"I like that. They'd be uniform and fairly small."

"I'd keep it simple: name, lot, and where they lived on our date."

"Okay, but I have to get that information from everyone in the park," Julie said. "Nan's got people knocking on my door asking to be my little helpers, and I don't know what to tell them."

An idea popped into my head. "What if we use this display thing to justify our whole investigation?"

Julie caught on immediately. "We give up on separate stories and collect the information directly."

"We can claim that was the plan all along. Nan spoiled the surprise, but you're thrilled that everyone is responding to it positively."

"That will resolve any suspicions people had about our odd questions over the last few days." Julie's energy seemed to flow back, and she sat up straight. "I'll have the volunteers cover the women, Canadians, and men too old or too young to be Greg Miles. The eight of us will keep our lists, but now we have a good reason to ask for specific information on that date."

"If you want, I'll organize the volunteers. You make the lists, and I'll see that they get them and do the work."

"Would you? That will free me from daily questions and let me start figuring out the map."

I looked at the calendar behind her. "With a squad of volunteers, I bet we can get the interviews done in a week. What do you think?"

Julie rose and held out her arms for a hug. "I think it's great to have friends like you and Wilma and Alice."

I hugged her back. "In this case, you should probably call us minions. But hey, that's what friends are for, right?"

Chapter Thirty-One

Julie (Ron & Julie) Sunday, 1:00 p.m.

If I had to choose who'd turn out to be the killer from Nashville, I'd have picked a guy a few trailers down from us, Del Hanna. The worst male chauvinist I've ever met, the guy hasn't got a clue why that's a bad thing. The first few times we met, I'd walk away when he started in, but I've gotten ornerier lately, and I call Del out. Ron gets embarrassed, and my comments make no dent in his massive ego, so it's a useless enterprise. Mostly I try to avoid being where he is.

Del was on Wilma's list, but she'd asked me to take him for follow-up. "He claims to have been living in Ohio in '67," she told me, "but he mentioned driving a truck, and he said he'd been to Nashville." Her face had turned pink as she added, "He's certainly the type who would have had a girlfriend in every town along the way."

"And the type who might force himself on a woman," I opined. To be fair, Del wasn't forcing his current "lady," the lovely Shawna, to do anything. In fact, rumor had it the opposite was true. Residents were snickering up their sleeves and saying Del had finally met his match.

When I questioned Wilma more closely, she said the truck was full of band equipment, and Del had traveled as a musician, not a semi driver. That didn't sound like our suspect, but it still required further investigation. Taking my clipboard and promising myself I'd be civil, I went down five lots to Del's place.

I'd never been inside, though I'd stopped to introduce myself to Shawna the day they arrived. They'd been unloading the car (Actually, Del was. Shawna was checking her phone.) Buxom and blond, she had a topically-applied kind of beauty, lots of makeup and a few surgical enhancements, if I had to guess. She was at least two decades younger than Del, and I wondered how he'd convinced her to spend five months with him in a trailer.

Since Del didn't remember my name, I had provided it, along with an offer to advise Shawna if she needed the name of a hair stylist or nearby stores with decent prices. She looked at me for a second, blinked mascara-laden eyes, and said, "O-kay." Her tone hinted that consulting me about anything was the last thing she could imagine doing.

Since then I'd been polite but not friendly. At my age, I don't pursue people who make it clear I'm not their cup of tea. From what I could tell, Shawna's interests were her nails, hair, and magazines that claim to present the secrets of Hollywood stars, starlets, and stinkers. She'd made a few friends in the park among others who live vicariously through celebrities. If I happened to be in her vicinity, I soon lost track of gossip about who Bradley is seeing this month and why Kim is so upset with her mom or her sister or whoever.

When I knocked on her door, Shawna answered, though that isn't a precise term. She came to the door and looked at me. No greeting. No "What can I do for you?" Not even "What do you want?"

"I'm working on a project for the park," I told her. "I'm asking everyone where they were in July of 1967. I plan to put the answers on a map, so we can all see where we were at a certain point in time."

She blinked eyelids so heavy with black stuff I wondered how they managed to reopen. "I was barely born then."

"That's okay," I said brightly. "Tell me where you were, and I'll put it on our map."

She didn't like the idea but apparently couldn't think of a reason to refuse. "Dilby, Mississippi."

"I haven't heard of it. Where's it located?"

"Right next to nowhere." Her voice was the equivalent of a sneer. "I got out as soon as I could."

"I see. Is Del around? I need to ask him the same question."

"Somebody asked him already. Some woman."

I looked at my list. "Oh. She must have forgotten to write it down."

Shawna stared as if trying to decide how big a lie it would take to get rid of me. Apparently it wasn't worth the effort of inventing one, and she said, "He's out riding his bike." She stepped back from the door. "You can wait if you want."

The interior of Del's trailer was man-cave, mitigated in pitifully small measure by beautification efforts from a succession of now-departed women. Neon beer signs stood in for lamps, and those horrible velvet paintings of mostly-naked women served as decoration. The furniture was dark oak upholstered in deep brown, so any light that entered was immediately sucked away.

Having known three of Del's former "ladies," I guessed that the colorful vase of fake tulips had been added by Debbie, the embroidered doily on the back of the recliner was the product of Jackie's skill with a needle, and the ceramic flamingo on the end table had been chosen by Helene from one of Florida's many dollar stores. Though all three women had been friendlier than Shawna, none had been able to control how Del treated them. He talked to his "ladies" as if they were stupid, ran around with other women when the chance arose, and let them pay the bills without a hint of guilt or a breath of thanks. Sooner or later, each one had given up trying. Del didn't mind; he simply went out and found a new woman to look down on.

After an awkward silence I asked, "Are you enjoying your stay in Florida, Shawna?"

Her brows dropped like twin seagulls on a dive. "Are you kidding? He made this place sound like there were big things happening all the time. Big things?" She made a disdainful *pfft!* with her lips. "Card games and spaghetti suppers." Sweeping a hand at the trailer she said, "He went on about 'my place on Flamingo Lake' like it was a friggin' mansion. I get here and find a metal box a mile away from the pool." Her tone dropped lower. "Which is the size of a postage-stamp, and the whole frigging park has to share it."

"We like B-Bird," I said stiffly. "It's low key and—"

Her laugh was like a rifle shot. "It's low-key all right." Bending, she picked up a magazine from an end table. On the cover, a celebrity I couldn't name showed off her…well, pretty much her whole self in a dress that almost wasn't there. Though Shawna didn't look down, her fingertips brushed the picture as if assuring herself that the world really is an exciting place for some. "Every morning, I wake up and remember where I am and want to scream."

Embarrassed by Shawna's angry face, I glanced away and noticed two blankets and sheet neatly folded at the foot of the futon. It appeared that Del was sleeping on the lanai as punishment for his deceit.

The sound of a kick-stand lowering indicated Del had arrived home. When he came inside and saw me, he did a double-take, and I guessed he wasn't used to company.

"This woman wants to ask you something," Shawna said. Turning, she disappeared into the back of the trailer, and a rumble indicated a sliding door rolling into place. More evidence the bedroom was no-man's-land these days.

Ignoring all that, I adopted a businesslike tone. "Del, you might have heard I'm doing a display of where everyone in the park was on a certain date. Can you tell me where you were on July 7, 1967?"

"Not specifically. I was in a different town every night."

"Can you give me a ballpark guess?"

"My home was in Ohio, outside Springfield. You can put that down for my answer."

A muted slam at the back of the trailer caught our attention, but everything went silent. "But you aren't sure you were there on that date?"

"I had a band, and we performed anywhere they'd let us, from the Atlantic shore to the Mississippi." His face took on a hopeful expression. "Maybe you heard of us. The Bucky Boys?"

"Um, no. did you ever go south, into Tennessee or Georgia?"

He frowned, "Yeah. Why?"

"No reason, but someone told me yesterday about two murders that took place in Nashville on that date. I wondered if you heard about it."

"No." I watched carefully, but Del didn't seem the least bit fazed by the information. "We played Nashville a few times, but I never paid attention to the local news. It's a lot of work setting up for a show, getting all your energy together for the crowd, and then striking the whole thing so you can move on in the morning."

"Did you have a girlfriend back at home?"

His laugh was cynical. "I had a wife. The first of four mistakes I made before I finally figured things out."

"Figured out what?"

"That when a man has the urge to get married, he should find a woman he doesn't like and buy her a house. The result is the same."

Glancing at the closed bedroom door, I reflected that Del wasn't getting great results now, even though he'd replaced the wives in his past with a never-ending string of "ladies."

Chapter Thirty-Two

Alice (Tommy & Alice) Sunday, 2:00 p.m.

Passing the open doorway to the laundry room, I saw Karen taking a load of blue jeans out of a washer. “Hey.”

“Hi, Alice.” She raised her thumbs in mock celebration. “Laundry. The height of my week.” After checking to make sure I was alone, she asked, “Are you helping Julie input the information for the display?”

“Yes. We should finish our interviews quickly now that we have a plausible reason for asking. We should have thought of it before.”

Her brows met briefly. “Still, it doesn’t mean our guy will tell the truth. If I were a double murderer, I’d lie like a rug.”

“All we can do is turn what we find out over to O’Connor. What he does with it will be up to him.”

“Speaking of the detective, Marlene told me the other day that their relationship is getting serious. Julie says O’Connor spoke as if they’re only dating casually.”

“Hmm. Sounds like he and our secretary are traveling on different wavelengths.” I waited while Karen opened a dryer and leaned in to load the wet clothes. “What do you think of the man?”

She checked the lint tray and made a disgusted face at the half-inch coat of fuzz clinging to its surface. “I only met him once, but I got an impression.” Cleaning the filter into the trash can, she banged it on the edge and then put it back in place. "Back in the day, we called guys like him *uptight*." Fishing quarters from her pocket, she started the dryer, adding, "Marlene likes him a lot though. You should see her face light up when she talks about him."

"Then I hope it works out for them."

Karen moved her basket to another dryer. "Me too."

I went on, but my thoughts remained on Marlene, who was too nice to ever give a man an ultimatum. My reading of her personality was that she'd smile and blush and put up indefinitely with a man's commitment avoidance. Was O'Connor playing around? Was he too shy to make a move? Had he been burned too many times? Whatever the holdup was, I had a feeling the relationship needed an intervention.

Admittedly, I'm the last person in the world who should play matchmaker. My track record with men is abysmal, at least it was for most of my life. Somehow, at sixty-eight, I stumbled onto Tommy, who is everything I'd convinced myself no man would ever be: kind, gentle, thoughtful, and—it took me a while to admit this—faithful. Once you find a mate like that, and once you admit you got really, really lucky, you wish other women could find Mr. Right too.

My friends don't fully understand how wonderful their marriages are. Living with a normal guy for forty, even fifty years, they have no idea how wrong things can go between couples. I'm sure Ron has never hit Julie. Wilma's probably never even heard Earl swear, much less had him shout curses directly into her ears. And the way Al looks at Karen, you'd think she was a goddess. None of them has to struggle against old fears of abuse, fight feelings of panic they can't control, or suppress anger they can't reason away.

They gripe about empty dishes left in the fridge and muddy shoes worn into the house. Sometimes I join in, since those things are part of living with another person. But I know the difference between little squabbles with your mate and deadly fear of him. I appreciate the love I get from my husband in a different way than my friends do. Slowly, I'm learning to let go of my fears and let my feelings show, to Tommy and to everyone else.

That's why Marlene's situation troubled me. When a man doesn't move forward in a relationship, all too often the reason is an existing marriage. With that on my mind, I headed for Julie's house. She knew the detective better than the rest of us. Besides, Ms. Retired Librarian can track information through cyberspace like a hound on a scent.

"You want to spy on a police detective?" she asked a few minutes later. "Alice, we've got tons of other things to work on, and besides that, it's not right."

"You need a break from the Miles thing. O'Connor is romancing Marlene but avoiding the question of where the relationship is headed. Shouldn't she know if he has a half-dozen kids somewhere?"

She kept refusing. I kept insisting. Finally, she agreed to look at O'Connor's social media profile. "Things he puts there are public," she said in a self-righteous tone, "so we aren't really snooping."

"That should work," I leaned over Julie's shoulder as she started typing. "These days, people under fifty who don't post pics are few and far between."

We found him on two sites, one designed for sharing photos and the other for business contacts. There were pics of O'Connor with a dark-haired woman, but they were over a year old. I learned that he liked playing basketball (no league, just pickup) and watching football (the Tampa Bay Buccaneers). A photo revealed he'd tried deep-sea fishing, but his grim expression and greenish-pale complexion hinted he hadn't had a great time.

On the business contacts site, he listed himself as single (not a guarantee) with no children. His profile sounded a little stiff, like O'Connor himself, but it was accurate as far as we could determine. He'd been a detective for a little over two years, and before that held a variety of law enforcement jobs from patrol officer to public relations representative.

I directed Julie back to the social site, where she scrolled farther into O'Connor's past. Three different women showed up in his pictures, all of them smiling happily as they clung to him. For one, a name came up when Julie hovered the cursor over her face. "Jennifer Bonafista," I urged. "How many women with that name can there be in Florida?"

Jennifer had a much more active social site than O'Connor did, and we found several pictures of them together. We found no evidence of an acrimonious break-up, but Jennifer started showing up with a new guy, one as handsome as O'Connor but maybe a touch warmer, pulling her close for the shots. Best of all we learned, since Jenni told all on social media, that she currently worked at a shop less than ten miles from B-Bird Park.

"You want to what?" Julie asked when I proposed my plan.

"Talk to this Jenni. We're shoppers. We're old ladies. We chat with salesclerks."

"I can't believe you want to intrude on O'Connor's personal life like that."

"Didn't you pretend to be shopping for real estate last month in order to find out what kind of person someone was?"

"Well yes, but we were looking for a criminal."

“It’s criminal to string some poor woman along. Do you want poor Marlene hanging out with some pretty-faced man who might be lying about who he is?”

Julie knows more than most about my abusive ex-husband, so she realized I was looking out for Marlene’s best interests. “Okay. We’ll go tomorrow, if you promise to be discreet. And careful.”

“Sure thing. Shall I drive, or will you?”

Chapter Thirty-Three

Wilma (Earl & Wilma) Monday 11:00 a.m.

When the clock showed 11:00 a.m. Monday morning, I started putting away my embroidery stuff, a floral panel with purple irises that would spruce up my niece's front door for spring. When you live in a trailer space is precious, so tools and materials need to be put away between work times. Storage space is limited too, so I'm careful about which crafts I bring to Florida each year. Sewing and quilting require a lot of room, so I do those in Michigan, where I have a large area to spread the bits and pieces out and leave them for as long as I need to. At B-Bird, I do smaller projects, like beading, crocheting, and embroidery.

The people who design trailers are clever about inserting shelves and drawers all over, but they're not always easy to get at. In our deeper closets I have tote bags for each craft packed like olives in a jar. To get to *Embroidery* that morning, I'd pulled out bags marked *Paints* and *Beading*. I store them with my current project in front, accessible for the next time I have a few minutes to work.

That done, I got ready to visit the nursing home. Once a week I go with Hank Edmonds to visit his wife, Janis. She doesn't know me anymore; in fact, she doesn't know much of anything. I think it's important to respect who she was, not what's left in her poor, diseased brain.

Hank picked me up right on time, and we left the quiet of B-Bird for the bustle of the city. As he drove Hank said, "Did you hear that Del's girlfriend took off?"

I don't like gossip, but Del had been on my mind lately. The way he'd been acting made me feel funny, like things were being said that weren't being said, if that makes sense. "I hadn't heard that."

"She arranged with the Uber guy to take her to the airport. When Julie stopped by to talk to Del, Shawna went out the back door, between the neighbors' trailers, and met the Uber car on the next street. Never said a word about it to Del." Hank touched the cigarette pack in his shirt pocket, which I guessed meant he wished he could smoke. "He talks like he knew she was fixin' to leave, but I have my doubts."

I didn't know whether that news was good or bad as far as my dealings with Del went. Being left behind might make the man realize that he didn't treat women very nicely. On the other hand, if Shawna had been unhappy for a while, the creepy feeling I'd been having when Del was around might mean he was looking for…I won't call it love. I hoped he didn't think he'd get what he wanted from me.

Our visit with Janis was like all the other times. Cheerful as could be, Hank fed her and talked to her as if she was the Janis of before. When I'm there, Hank and I pretend she's listening and tell stories about people and events in the park. When she was first admitted to the facility, Janis would listen and nod, at least sometimes. These days she stares into space, not even aware we're in the room.

When we leave, Hank's always a little sad. I don't claim to know God's purpose in letting good people suffer. All I can do is listen when he talks about Janis the way she was.

Hank was the last man on my interview list, so when we left Janis sitting in a wheelchair and headed to his car I asked, "Where did the two of you meet?"

Hank adjusted the rear view mirror before replying. "Little Rock, Arkansas. Janis was born and raised there."

"And when did you move to Little Rock?"

"Oh, I don't know." He adjusted the mirror again before backing out of the space. "Spring of '67, maybe."

"How'd you end up there?"

He didn't answer for a few seconds. "Kind of landed there, I guess. I'd been kicking around a while, six days on the road most weeks, but I found a good job at a factory in Little Rock. A while later I met Janis, and I wasn't going anywhere after that."

"Was she your first love?"

Hank frowned. "First real one. You don't know who really loves you till things get tough."

Something in Hank's tone stayed on my mind. That night while Earl and me were playing cards, I told him what Hank had said. "He didn't say he was a trucker, but isn't that how they say it? Six days on the road?"

"There's a song that says it that way," Earl said, "but he could have been in sales or some other job that requires travel."

"Hank isn't Greg Miles," I said firmly. "I mean, he stretches the truth sometimes, but he'd never kill anyone."

"Right," Earl agreed. "No way Hank is the guy."

Chapter Thirty-Four

Julie (Ron & Julie) Monday 12:00 p.m.

I will never figure out how I let myself be talked into meeting Detective O'Connor's old girlfriend, but in my defense, Alice can be a bit of a steamroller. I worked until ten Monday morning on what had become simply "The Project" in my mind, trying to get a handle on how I'd fit hundreds of bits of information onto a map mounted on poster board. It would have to be more than one sheet, I decided. Maybe four. I left my configurations when Alice came out of her trailer, waved, and started the car. Grabbing my purse, I went out to join her.

We entered the Miracle Mall on Sunset Drive and turned right at a sign that said Dream Escapes was that way. The store turned out to be one of those "Oh, my!" lingerie places, and I glanced around, hoping no one I knew saw me go inside. As I tried to ignore the scantily clad mannequins and tables laid with "Oh my goodness!" merchandise, Alice ordered, "Keep the blonde clerk busy. I'll see what the ex has to say."

I'd recognized Jenni right away, though she was coiffed and dressed more elegantly than the beach shots she'd posted. She was behind the desk, peering at a computer screen. Her name tag identified her as the store manager.

The other woman glanced up at us, set down her phone, and asked, "How can I help you?"

"I need a—um, I'd like to look at…" What? I'd never worn such skimpy underwear, and at my age it was silly to pretend I might.

"She needs a gift for her granddaughter's bridal shower," Alice supplied. "We were thinking a teddy."

"Cool." Blondie set her phone down and came out from behind the counter. "Do you know her size?"

"Medium."

"Perfect. Open crotch or crotch-less?"

That stopped me for a moment. "Do they come with crotches?"

"Sure." She led me to a table laden with garments that looked as if the seamstress had gone to lunch without finishing them. "These two have crotches, but the boobs are out." I must have looked horrified, because she went on to another stack. "These may be more what you're thinking of."

I hadn't been thinking of anything even close, but I managed to look interested as she lauded the various choices, sheerness, color, level of "attraction." She didn't mention durability, which is something I look for in underwear. Probably not a selling point here.

When Alice finally came to join me, I told the clerk I needed to keep looking. "I'll probably be back for the green one," I said. She smiled at the familiar lie and faded back to her spot behind the counter, where she took up her phone and promptly forgot us.

"I hope that was worth the embarrassment I suffered," I told Alice when we'd left the store.

"Every bit," she replied. "Let's have ice cream for lunch, and I'll tell you all about Detective O'Connor."

I ordered the smallest sundae on the menu. Alice doesn't need to worry about what ice cream will do to her hips, but since menopause hit and changed everything about me, I do. As we sat at a small table with those cute but uncomfortable wire-backed chairs, she passed on what she'd learned.

"I told Miss Jenni how you were recently in the news because you helped catch a killer. I casually mentioned that the detective on the case, Ray O'Connor, said you were instrumental in solving the crime."

"And she reacted to the name."

"Of course she did." Alice licked her cone where ice cream had begun running down the side. "Jenni and Ray were an item for about a year. They never moved in together, but he stayed over at her place quite often, and they were…What's the term? Exclusive."

"What went wrong?"

"Nothing specific. Ray was considerate and easy to be with. He tolerated her cats—she has three—and was great with her parents and younger brother. But after a while Jenni realized there wasn't any spark. They were okay together but not great. I got the impression that Ray can be…emotionally distant. Jenni wanted more, and she claims she's found it with a guy named Paolo."

"And how did O'Connor take that?"

"Like a gentleman. In fact, Jenni suspects he was waiting for her to break up with him."

"Why would he do that?"

"Jenni's known O'Connor for years, and she says he kind of floats along in a relationship, putting off commitment until the woman gives up and moves on." She licked at the cone. "One would hope if he really loved someone, he'd fight to keep her, but so far, that hasn't happened."

I finished my teeny-tiny bowl of butter pecan. "Does that convince you that O'Connor isn't some womanizer who's lying to

Marlene?"

"We know he's a decent guy," Alice replied. "It's up to her to either pull him in or push him away."

"And how would she do that?" I grinned. "It's been a long time since I had to plot how to get a guy to make a commitment."

"It's different for everybody," Alice said, "I'd say Marlene has to do something that shows him she has options. If he doesn't step up, she'll know she doesn't mean that much to him."

"She needs to give him a shove and see what happens."

"Exactly," Alice said. "If it's nothing, she'll be sad, but at least she'll see that her faint hope isn't going to turn into hearts and flowers."

Chapter Thirty-Five

Earl (Earl & Wilma) Monday, 1:30 p.m.

At one-thirty, I went inside to tell Wilma it was almost time to go to shuffleboard. She was still wearing the outfit she'd worn when visiting Janis, and she said she wanted to change into something cooler. She'd be ready in ten minutes. Now, every guy in the world knows that ten minutes to a woman is like ten minutes left in a football game. Stuff that happens in between doesn't count toward the actual ten minutes it takes to change her shirt and shoes. I call her my little slowpoke, but it's always worth the wait.

My Wilma is still a looker. Yeah, we've gotten older, but she has a beautiful complexion and great big eyes that make you want to stare into them. She gripes about age spots and gray hairs mixed in with the blond, but when I look at her, I only see that girl I fell in love with more than fifty years ago.

Lately, Wilma's been a little irritable. She hints that I fuss too much, but I'm only trying to show how important she is to me. Some guys kind of ignore their wives after years and years, and I don't ever want Wilma to think anything could take her place. I show interest in things she likes to do, even though it's hard sometimes. I don't sing, so choir is out. I tried Bible study, but I dozed off near the end, which embarrassed her. I didn't mean for it to happen, but how many ways can you slice up something as simple as "Love thy neighbor"? They went on for two hours about who your neighbor is, when to me there's no discussion. Jesus never said to anybody, "Go away, you're not my neighbor," at least not that I can find in the Bible.

Another thing that makes Wilma's forehead pucker is me trying to keep her safe. She's no bigger than a minute, so she'd never be able to fight off an attacker. In addition to that, she's lived a pretty sheltered life. On the farm no one threatened her—except a rooster we had years ago, and he got to be Sunday dinner. Wilma thinks the best of everyone, which is a tribute to her Christian spirit and loving heart. Still, we all need to recognize that not everyone in the world has good intentions. The murder in the park had left me wondering when another bad person might show up at B-Bird, and I didn't want anyone to do my beautiful girl harm.

Wilma was ready to go in only twenty minutes. As we walked to the court together, I explained the new plan Ron come by to tell me that morning. "We're all supposed to be helping Julie make this big display that will show where everyone at B-Bird was on July 7, 1967."

"That's certainly easier than trying to twist a conversation around to finding it out," she said. "It felt like I was making pretzels."

We went on, greeting friends as we passed. When we first came to B-Bird it was odd to see no familiar faces, but now we know lots of people. Many Michiganders "fly" south to escape the snow and cold, so when we gave up the farm, we decided to try it. Our niece found us a trailer to rent for three months, and we made it a point to stop and chat here and there when we walked in the evenings. Later, people began stopping at our place too. The second year we bought a park model and stayed a month longer. I signed up for some teams, and Wilma joined the choir. Now lots of people know Earl and Wilma from Michigan.

At the shuffleboard court, I joined the men who were getting out the cues and pucks. Wilma sat down on a bench in the shade. The last player to arrive was Archie from Stork Street. His buddy Lloyd drove their golf cart. He remained seated as Arch hurried forward, muttering an apology for being late. When I saw Wilma get up and stroll over to Lloyd, I knew what she was up to. Lloyd and Archie were on my list, and she figured it was a good time to check them off. I considered bowing out of the first game to help, but there were only enough guys to fill the teams. Besides, Arch and Lloyd would be easy. Since they don't care for girls, it isn't likely either of them was ever a rapist. They're at the upper end of the age limit too, being in their mid-eighties. Wilma didn't even glance my way, so I figured she didn't mind being on her own. It would be easy now, since all she had to do was say we were helping Julie with her map thing. That was a lot better than telling whoppers.

As we took our places at opposite ends of the court, I heard Wilma's greeting to Lloyd. "Hasn't the Lord sent us a beautiful day?" After that we started the game, and I couldn't hear the conversation for the scrape of sticks and the cheers of the players. Lloyd and Wilma talked almost the whole time we played.

During the last round, Wilma gave Lloyd a pat on the arm and started back to the bench. She stopped and turned when someone called her name. Coming toward her was Del Hanna, wearing a smile I'd have to call slimy. Though Wilma smiled back, she crossed her arms, as if she was cold. As they stood there talking, I got distracted from the game. Someone had to remind me I was up, and my shot was way too hard and went off the back of the triangle, losing the game for our side. It's a good thing our matches are only for fun. The guys gave me a little grief for sloppy play, but that was all.

I helped with the clean-up, but I kept an eye on Del and Wilma. After what seemed like a long time, she backed away from him, her arms still crossed. When she turned, Wilma saw me watching and blushed, like she'd been caught doing something bad. My blood pressure rose a little, at least that's how it felt. A guy never knows what Del might be up to when there's a woman involved.

Once the equipment was packed away, we said our goodbyes and started for home. “What did Del Hanna want?”

“We’re doing a duet for church,” she replied. “He suggested some extra practice.”

“A tough one, huh?”

She hesitated. “I didn’t think so, but he acts like it needs work.”

I had an inkling what old Del was thinking. “If he’s bothering you, let me know. I’ll have a word with the guy.”

“You don’t need to do that, Earl.” There was that irritation again. I’d tried to help and instead made her mad at me. “We’ll practice. We’ll sing the song. It’ll be fine.”

I gave it a minute before asking, “How’d it go with Lloyd?”

“He and Arch have been together since 1965.” Wilma’s voice was cool. “Neither of them ever did any trucking. Lloyd was a millwright and Archie worked at a hospital. They’ve never been to Nashville except to drive through it.”

I tried to do some fence-mending. “Seems like you’re a pretty slick investigator, Wilma.”

She sniffed away the compliment. “I think it’s mean, spying on our friends, but if there’s a murderer living here, I suppose it’s our duty to find him if we can.”

Chapter Thirty-Six

Karen (Al & Karen)-Monday, 1:00 p.m.

Julie asked me to do follow-up on Matthew Nowicki. A guy Ron talked to said he'd met Matthew in Connecticut in 1967, so either Wilma had been too vague with her questions or he'd lied to her.

To grease the wheels a little, I took along a couple of pieces of a cake I'd made. You'd have thought I gave them two gold bars.

"That's so nice of you," Taffy said. "Tomorrow's our anniversary, so we can have cake to celebrate."

"Really," I said. "How many years?"

"Forty-six," Matthew said with obvious pride. "We have a very strong marriage."

"We've been a couple a lot longer than that," Taffy put in. "It took me forever to get Matthew to the altar."

"We weren't really a couple until we took vows before God, Taffy." As usual when he spoke to her, his voice took on an "I have to talk down to this silly woman" tone.

Taffy wasn't deterred in the least. "I know, but I was sure you were the one when we were in high school, so I count our time from then."

I turned to Matthew. "I thought you grew up in the Philippines."

"My parents were missionaries with the AG church. Dad was very popular over there. He even met President Marcos a couple of times." His lips pursed briefly, which I recognized as Matthew in Boast Mode. "I did my schooling totally through correspondence, because Dad said I needed an American education, not some watered-down Filipino version. I finished all my courses in the spring of 1970." He added a characteristic repetition. "Totally through correspondence."

"If you lived in the Philippines, how did you two meet?"

Taffy was eager to explain. "We started as pen pals. Matthew's aunt was my Sunday school teacher, and she was always talking about her brilliant missionary nephew, so I asked if I could write to him."

"I'm an excellent correspondent," Matthew put in. "Lots of girls wanted to know what it was like to live in a strange place and do the Lord's work." He smirked. "Of course they always wanted a photo."

"Matthew came home to visit one summer," Taffy said. "I went right up to him at our church picnic and said, 'I'm Taffy, and I've been writing to you.'" She tittered, adding, "Remember what you said, Matthew? 'You and half the girls in Connecticut.'"

What girl could resist such charm? Aloud I said, "What year was that?"

Taffy considered. "It was 1967. The year I won Runner Up in the Miss Middletown Pageant."

To Matthew I said, "And did you have a job while you were home for the summer?"

"I did. I've always been a worker; you can ask anyone. I got a job driving truck."

"So young?"

"I'd been driving since I was thirteen, and the only vehicle at our compound was an old army Deuce-and-a-Half. If a guy could drive that, he could handle anything."

I wanted to ask what sort of driving he'd done, but Taffy took over the conversation, giving me a blow-by-blow description of their first meeting. I left convinced Matthew couldn't be our guy. As I told Julie later, "I can't imagine a kid his age got a real truck-driving job. He probably made local deliveries."

"Yeah," Julie said. "And Connecticut is a long way from Arizona, so I don't see how Matthew could have stolen Greg Miles' ID." Raising her brows she asked, "Do we cross him off the list?"

"I think we have to. To be fair, being annoying doesn't make a person a killer."

"No." Julie's voice revealed disappointment. "That's the problem. Nobody here seems like the killer type—whatever that might be."

Chapter Thirty-Seven

Julie (Ron & Julie) Monday, 8:00 p.m.-Tuesday, 9:00 a.m.

One of the great tests of marriage is respect for your partner's things. Sadly, there's no predicting when those tests will arise. I'm used to being chided for not showing enough love to our vehicles, which I consider to be Ron's job. Isn't it more efficient if one person takes responsibility for filling the gas tanks, washing the exterior, and applying whatever stuff is required to keep the seats and dashboard looking good? Ron considers the inside of the house my domain (at least when he's not recuperating from surgery), so I'm a little resentful when I'm urged to "come outside and see how good the car looks." Do I make him approve the recently scrubbed toilet or the shine I put on the wood floor in the lanai? No.

While his vehicle and his power tools are carefully handled and kept in pristine condition, Ron views electronic devices as toys and treats them as such. He's had two screens replaced due to his practice of shoving his phone into the leg pocket of his cargo shorts, where it often connects with hard surfaces like support posts and golf cart sides. Once he lost the phone completely when he knelt to look at the lie of a golf ball. Luckily, some honest soul turned it in, muddy and damp, and I was able to revive it with rice and a lot of TLC. His carelessness with his "toy" irritates me, since I'm the one who's expected to work a miracle and fix it.

Ron's relaxed attitude extends to my devices as well. Monday evening I asked him to hand me my tablet, and he tossed it—literally tossed it at me like a Frisbee. As he knows perfectly well, I've never in my life caught anything thrown my way. "Ron," I said as I retrieved it from the couch cushions, "do you realize you're throwing around a delicate instrument that's priced at a thousand dollars?"

He was immediately defensive. "It wasn't even that far." The remark was quickly followed by a counterattack. "You're the one who opens the drapes like you're on the Harvard tug-of-war team."

A response to that would only escalate things, so I opened my email and read for a while. Seeing a coupon for the bookstore I asked, "Are we going shopping when you get back from golf tomorrow?"

"We probably should. I'm almost out of peanuts."

Now there's a food emergency.

When Ron left with Earl Tuesday morning, I headed to beading class. It's a new thing for me, and I'm afraid it's not a good fit, but I promised myself I'd try it for six weeks. The instructor is patient, so it's fun, even if I can't imagine myself ever producing anything but single-strand jewelry.

As we work we talk, and a woman at my table did more than her share. We heard about her various ailments in more detail than necessary, though she did seem to have a lot to deal with. She'd educated herself on medications that combated each of her illnesses, and her use of terms like "oxy" and "NSAIDs" sounded more like a DEA agent than a person stringing beads on wire. I tuned out after a while, focusing on the pattern I'd chosen, five tiny white beads then two larger red carnelians with a mid-sized black onyx between.

I tuned in again when someone asked the woman, "Did you call the pharmacy and tell them they shorted you?"

"They insist they didn't," she replied. "The tech said they're very careful, because they have to account to the government for every pill dispensed." Raising pencil-thin brows, she added an opinion. "They weren't that careful, or I wouldn't have eight pills in a ten-pill bottle."

She went off on a theme that's all too familiar among people of a certain age. "In my day, when we took a job, we did it right. It's not like that anymore." With a derisive sniff she finished, "Nowadays, no one understands what the word *responsibility* means."

I stayed quiet, but I have a more realistic view on that subject, or perhaps a better memory. Over the years that I worked at the library, there were always employees who made every effort to avoid doing their jobs. They slacked. They did things half-way. They hid in the stacks and played kissy-face. Librarians are some of society's best people, in my opinion, so if they come in motivated and not-so-motivated types, then all workers do and always did. Memory is a tricky thing though. In hindsight, you convince yourself that life was better when you were young, healthy, and able.

Ron and I spent the afternoon out and about, buying supplies and adding to our store of things we don't actually need. I wanted a new rug for the kitchen, but I was well aware it wasn't a necessity. It's simply nice to have goals to work toward.

As we crossed a parking lot, a truck pulled up nearby and stopped with a hiss of brakes. I didn't pay much attention, but Ron, a former logger, is fascinated by the operation of any large piece of machinery. We waited, watching the driver maneuver the truck until it was precisely where he needed it to be.

"Can't imagine putting one of those monsters into these tight little spaces," he remarked. "Out in the woods it doesn't matter if you clip a tree trunk, but here, anything you hit is gonna be a big deal."

"I'm sure it takes a lot of practice to get good at it."

Ron turned to look at me. "That's what he said."

"He who?"

"Hank Edmonds." Frowning, he dredged a story from his memory. "One day a bunch of us were talking about trucks and bulldozers and whatever, and Hank said driving a semi through a city was the most nerve-wracking thing a guy would ever have to do." I waited, sensing there was more, and Ron finished, "But the other day when I mentioned trucking, he said he never drove a big rig."

"What does that mean?"

"Not sure."

"Did he say he'd done it? If he only commented that it would be nerve-wracking, it would."

"But the way he said it made it sound like he knew what he was talking about."

We reached the store and Ron opened the door for me. "I hope Hank isn't getting dementia, like Janis," I said. "That would be too sad."

"Forgetting what you used to do for a living?" Ron shook his head. "I don't think that's how dementia works."

"Well, either he's driven a semi or he hasn't. He was on Wilma's list, and she cleared him, but I could have someone else re-check. What do you think?"

"Maybe." Ron pointed toward the sign that said "Home Living." "Right now it's essential that we find a rug that matches your blue kitchen curtains."

While we were out, I bought materials for the project: poster board, push pins, yarn, and markers. After dinner, I left Ron to do the dishes and took my stuff to the billiard room. As far as I can tell, nobody in the park plays pool, though I've seen a few grandkids in there during Christmas or winter break, I think out of bored desperation. B-Bird isn't exactly an adolescent's paradise. Not only do they have to sleep on air mattresses on the floor and share one tiny bathroom with their parents and grandparents, but the park itself has little to interest them other than the occasional alligator sighting. Trips to Disney and other tourist sites are usually part of the visit, but there's a lot of down time too. They hang out in the pool, even when the temperatures aren't conducive to a pleasant swim. They ride around on three-wheel bikes they wouldn't be caught dead on at home. Even our internet is weaker than what they're used to, and it's spotty too. Staying with Gram and Gramps at B-Bird probably isn't what "Let's go to Florida" initially calls to adolescent minds.

Luckily, the kids were back in school, and the billiard room was deserted. I could lay out my sheets of poster board and try to figure out how to get all the information tucked in somewhere. Most locations would be in the U.S. and Canada, but on a world map, that section would be too small to fit everyone in. Still, I had to have places to put people like Matthew, who'd been in the Philippines, and those like Tommy and Earl, who were in the military at the time.

The thought of Matthew made me pause. We didn't know for certain where he'd been on July 7th, but that was true for most of the stories we were hearing. Actual proof was in short supply, which was disheartening. I wanted to come through for Detective O'Connor, but in all likelihood, we were going to have to hand him a list of maybes.

I turned my mind back to the display. I needed to order a map, but what size should it be? After a few more anguished moments, I called Wilma. "Have you got time to come down to the billiard room? I need your advice."

She arrived in only a few minutes, since their place is close. When she opened the door, I caught a glimpse of Earl watching from their carport, his round face concerned. Recalling her comment about how paranoid he'd been since the murder, I guessed he didn't like her leaving the house after dark. Though a lot of husbands at B-Bird were probably more vigilant now, Earl has always treated Wilma like she's a delicate flower. I'd have told him to back off, but she's nicer than I am. I suppose we adjust to our spouses in our own ways through the years.

"What do you need, Julie?"

As I told her my concerns about the display, Wilma listened carefully, eying the poster board as I gestured to indicate how I imagined the final result. When I finished, she was silent for a moment. Then she said, "How set are you on using poster board as your base?"

I shrugged. "It's what came to mind when I thought of a display."

"Earl's got a couple of 4x8 sheets of leftover foam insulation in the shed. If we set one of those on a couple of the easels from the art room, you'd have a bigger space to work with."

"That's a great idea," I said. "I could fit a really big world map on that." Wilma bit her lip, as if she didn't want to contradict me. "What?"

"Well, you need the most space for the U.S. and Canada, right? Could you make the rest of the world smaller?" When I looked confused, she explained, "Get two maps, a big one of the Northern Hemisphere and a smaller one of the world. We'll cut them out and put the big one in the center. Then we'll add pieces of the smaller one around it."

"I get it. Asia on the left and Europe and Africa on the right. Wilma, that's brilliant. We won't have that many to locate on the small pieces, and we'll have the room we need for everyone else."

"Right." Wilma looked at the wall as if picturing the finished product. "I have some sari fabric in blues and greens that would make a nice background. It's plenty big enough to cover a 4x8 sheet."

"Where did you get sari fabric?"

She grinned. "You'd be amazed at what you can find at Salvation Army stores."

I set my hands on my hips. "Okay. So I get the maps. We cut them out and attach them to our base. I print off a label with each person's information, and we stick them around the outside. Then we run yarn from each label to the spot where each person was in 1967."

"If you don't mind, I could fasten something pretty to the outside border, so it makes a frame for the display."

"If I don't mind? Wilma, you're fantastic."

Her face went pink. "I like making things look nice."

"Well, go for it," I told her. "Make it as pretty as you like, and I'll make it as accurate as I can."

Chapter Thirty-Eight

Al (Al & Karen) Tuesday, 10:00 a.m.

Avery Goode put his foot on the rung of the chair next to him and leaned his own chair onto its back legs. "Al, there's a lot of people in this world who don't care much about the rest of us."

"True," I agreed. I'd asked him where he was in July of '67, and that apparently triggered a story.

"In 1966 I got hired to manage a small apartment building in Elmira, New York. Twenty units, all ground level. I did the on-site stuff for this businessman who owned the place. It was a good deal for me, since I could work at my day job and live rent-free." Avery stroked his mustache before adding, "I learned more about people in the five years I spent there than you'd ever want to know."

"Lesson number one: Some tenants are a pain in the keister."

He pointed at me. "Exactly. The twenty-somethings you excuse with 'He's young,' or 'She doesn't get it yet.' For them, kids renting for the first time, it was a matter of knocking on the door and laying down the law. But my first ever tenant from hell, Ethel, was sixty if she was a day. Anyone that age knows that when people get shoved together into a space, they need to consider what's good for everybody, but Ethel was too selfish—or maybe too dumb—to care.

"She came along in the fall of '66, when I was still new to the job. She seemed like a nice lady, and she passed the background check the owner ran on her. Around Christmas time, she moved her son Charlie in. He was a little slow, but he did the heavy lifting while his mother fed him and paid the bills. It ain't unusual."

"We've got a few here with the same arrangement."

Avery nodded and went on with his story. "The winter went okay. They covered the windows of the apartment with bedsheets, which didn't make me happy, but Miller Apartments wasn't exactly high-rent real estate. I figured she was probably on a skimpy budget, so I let it go.

"It was when the weather broke in the spring that Ethel became a real problem. First, she had Charlie drag this rusty old patio set in from somewhere, the dump, maybe, and set it outside their door. Then they added other stuff she called 'outdoor décor,' peace signs, five of the seven Disney dwarves, and three different Madonna statues. Since they sat outside to smoke, they set rusty coffee cans on the windowsills for the butts and ashes. The place looked like the set for *Sanford and Son*.

"Sounds like some lots around here," I put in, and he nodded again.

"It ain't easy, being a manager. You start by telling them nicely to clean the place up, but there isn't much of a stick to go with the carrot. You can assess fines, but what if they don't pay them? It's hard to tell an older person you're going to kick her out, knowing she's got nowhere else to go."

"A tough situation for you."

Avery nodded. "I talked Ethyl into getting rid of most of the mess out front, but then another problem got brought to my attention. Ethel was a tender-hearted type, and she'd started feeding the local wildlife. She scattered grain on the lawn to encourage Canada geese to stop by on their way north." He shook his head. "You know what those critters leave behind. Tenants couldn't walk on the grass without stepping in gook. She also set out dishes of food for stray cats, raccoons, foxes, and even a bobcat, according to the guy who came in to complain. Now, I never saw any bobcats, but the animals definitely figured out where the easy food was coming from. When I warned Ethyl to stop, she put the food out at night and took it back inside every morning."

Avery paused, and I said, "You had to evict her."

"Yeah. I felt bad, but the tenants were up in arms, and Ethel refused to listen to reason." Avery shifted in his chair as he came to the answer to my original question. "It was July when I filed the papers. I waited until Friday the 7th, because I didn't want to ruin her Fourth of July week. It gave her time to find a new place by August, even if the court granted her a grace period."

"You felt bad for her."

"I did. A few tenants complained about the 'sweet old lady' in Building A losing her home, but most were relieved to see the pair of them gone."

"Where did they go?"

Avery sighed. "I helped her find a place at a trailer park, and I talked real serious to her about abiding by their rules." He sniffed once. "I never heard how that worked out, but my problems didn't end there. Once Ethyl and Charlie were gone, we found a family of possums living in the crawlspace under their apartment." Avery raised a hand. "Don't ask me how they got there, but Charlie had torn up a big section of the floor trying to scare them away. Some outside climbing plant had taken advantage of the hole and grown up the inside wall." He gave me a half-grin. "Ethyl must have liked it, because there were little American flags tucked in among the leaves."

"What a mess."

He sighed. "All that outside junk I'd objected to? They'd moved it inside, rust, mud, mold, and all. We ended up gutting the whole apartment, replacing two walls and all the carpeting. First, I had to call in an exterminator to remove the possums and make sure there weren't any other critters in there, like rats." His nose wrinkled. "You can't imagine the smell."

I repeated my earlier comment. "A mess."

Avery was silent for a moment. "When people gripe about George and the rules here at B-Bird, I always recall how hard I tried to work with Ethel and Charlie, and how little it helped. Those two taught me it's best to make rules and then stick with them." He grinned, aware that his answer had been longer than it needed to be. "And now you know more than you ever wanted to about where I was in July of 1967."

Chapter Thirty-Nine

Earl (Earl & Wilma) Wednesday, 3:30 p.m.

Wilma came home from choir practice really quiet, and after about an hour she said, "Earl, I need to tell you something, but you've got to promise not to get mad."

Now what kind of a thing is that for a wife to say to her husband? I don't get mad, at least not very darned often, and in my opinion, telling somebody not to get mad is a good way to start him down the mad road.

"I'll try, Wilma. What is it you need to say?"

"You know Del Hanna, right? He sings in the choir and—"

"I know him," I interrupted.

"Well, like I told you, he and I were supposed to practice our duet for church. I'm doing the soprano, the melody, and he's got this part that echoes everything I say but with different—"

She was stalling, so I interrupted again. "What happened?"

"I thought he'd asked Anita to come early, but when I got there, it was only Del." She licked her lips. "He said we didn't need her to play for us, and that's is true. He can play both parts and sing too, so it wasn't—"

More stalling. "What did he do?"

A frown creased her forehead. "He was playing, and I was singing, and he said I should sit down on the bench beside him so he could hear me better. I did, but it felt funny."

I'll bet it did. It felt like my blood pressure was rising, but I managed to nod as if I wasn't picturing myself tearing the guy's arm off and beating him over the head with it.

"Then he put his arm around me, kind of like he was showing me something, but…" Reliving it, Wilma grew angry. "Earl, I stood up right away, and I told him off. I said, 'Del Hanna, you can have all the 'ladies' you can get to put up with you in your life, but no decent woman would give you the time of day.'"

"Then what?"

She looked surprised, like I should have known. "Why, I left him sitting there. I went outside and waited until some of the others came to practice, and then I went in with them. I didn't speak to Del or look at him, but I told Ronda that I wasn't going to be able to do the duet." She shivered. "Even thinking about singing with that…creep gives me goose bumps."

I felt a surge of relief. I felt proud of my wife. I felt ready to track down Hanna and… Wilma pointed a finger at my nose. "Remember, you promised not to get mad."

"Wilma—"

"Earl, we have to live in this park. We don't want to start a feud."

"Nobody I know would take Del's side."

"Maybe not, but people love to talk. Some would say I should have known better than to go there and meet him."

"But he drew you there under false pretenses."

She rubbed at her forehead. "When I think of exactly what he said, I can't recall anything about Anita being there. I assumed she'd be, because that's how you or I would arrange something like that. We'd be careful of appearances and reputations and…feelings."

As I opened my mouth for another but, Wilma went on. "I want you to promise to let it go. I let Del know exactly how I felt, and I doubt he'll try anything with me again. I'll tell Ronda privately that I never want to sing with him. She'll understand."

My gut said it wasn't enough, but she added, "I didn't tell you this to make you mad at Del. I told you because I don't think there should be secrets between man and wife."

She was right. When I'd seen Del trying to snuggle up to Wilma, I'd wondered if she liked it. Now I knew she didn't. No matter how embarrassed she was about the incident, she'd kept me in the loop.

She'd also put old Del Hanna in his place. Maybe Wilma isn't as defenseless as I thought.

Chapter Forty

Julie (Ron & Julie) Wednesday, 4:00 p.m.

Wilma and Karen had both had a stab at pinning Matthew Nowicki down, but the question didn't feel finished to me. Alice was convinced he had secrets. "When did he really leave the Philippines?" she asked. "Taffy isn't the sharpest needle in the sewing box, so it wouldn't have been difficult for him to fool her. If they didn't get married until '74, what was he doing all those years?"

I had to agree, at least partially. If Matthew had been a truck driver, it was conceivable he'd gone as far as Arizona on a run and picked up Greg Miles' identity. It was disconcerting to think along those lines, because if he'd lied to Taffy about going back overseas, he must have had reasons that didn't bear thinking about.

"We need to get to the truth of Matthew's story," I said.

Alice nodded. "He's been making nice with Tommy lately, but I'm not ready to bury the hatchet. You're It."

When I knocked on Matthew's door, he stepped outside, inviting me to sit at the patio table. I noticed, not for the first time, that his favorite color is purple. The house is trimmed in purple. The patio chairs have purple seats. There are figurines hanging all around the carport frame: birds, fairies, fish, and elves, all purple. The driveway is painted purple. Don't ask me where you get purple paint for concrete. I have no idea.

"I need to check something with you," I told Matthew once we'd gotten past the pleasantries. "As you know, I'm asking everyone where they were on July 7, 1967, and I've got conflicting information." Feeling prissy I went on, "I'd like the display to be correct, so I came to ask in person."

Taffy came outside and sat down next to her husband. "I know where I was: working at the A&W in Middletown, Connecticut."

"Where exactly is that?"

"It's in the middle of the state, silly. Middle. Town. Get it?"

"Right. It's Matthew's information that's confusing. Wilma put the Philippines down as your residence, but Karen says you were in Connecticut that summer."

"I was," he replied. "My parents sent me home to look at colleges." He sniffed derisively. "I visited a few, but I didn't like what I saw. I agreed with Spiro Agnew that our nation's institutions of higher learning are filled with effete, intellectual snobs."

"So you went back to the Philippines?"

"Yes. I set about educating myself, reading widely and drawing my own conclusions rather than letting my head be filled with nonsense."

I disagreed, though not out loud. "But you were in the states in July."

"Yes."

"And on the seventh of the month? Where were you then?"

"At my aunt's, I suppose."

"No, you weren't," Taffy put in. "You went somewhere for a whole week, remember? You missed some of the Fourth of July stuff." She put on a pout. "You didn't tell where you were, like it was a big secret."

"It wasn't important." Matthew turned to me. "My permanent place of residence that year was the Philippines. I can show you where our mission was on a map if you like." Typically, he added, "Permanent place of residence."

Chapter Forty-One

Ron (Ron & Julie) Thursday, 8:00 a.m.

Del Hanna caught me at the pancake breakfast on Thursday. "Your wife asked me about a date for that poster thing she's doing." Julie was standing behind the serving counter, but according to Hank, Del's newest girlfriend had left without a word of goodbye. With his ego recently roughed up and knowing Julie isn't his biggest fan, Del no doubt found it easier to talk to me.

"Yes," I said. "We're almost done gathering information."

"I couldn't give her a location, since I was on the road a lot back then with my band, but later I realized I do know where I was that day." Del's expression showed a hint of pride as he explained, "July eighth is my oldest son's birthday. I was at a gig up north somewhere, but my mother-in-law tracked me down on the seventh to let me know my wife had gone into labor. I borrowed a car, drove all night, and managed to get back to Springfield in time for his arrival in the world at three a.m."

"That's good," I told him. "Julie will be pleased to know we have accurate information."

He snickered. "Just like a woman, huh? Always gotta pin you down."

I played along to keep him talking. "If she were here, she'd ask you to prove it."

"I could if I had to," Del replied. "My wife must have guessed the marriage wasn't going to last, because she made me sign what's called an acknowledgment of paternity." He made a disgusted huff before continuing. "I was the one who should have worried, not her. With me on the road all the time, he could have been anybody's kid."

Gee, I hope your wife appreciated your faith in her.

"I'm glad I signed though," Del went on. "David looks exactly like me, and he's the best thing I ever contributed to this world."

"What does he do?"

Del's chin rose. "He's with the Foreign Service. Mostly he works to keep the Middle East from blowing up."

I could almost hear Julie's comment. *If your son is a diplomat, he can't be much like his father.*

"Darla," Del said, and it took me a second to realize he was saying the name of his first wife. "We married young, and I thought that was it. You found a woman you could tolerate, and you lived with her. But no, that didn't suit Darla. She wanted— I don't know what she wanted. Some fairy tale life, I suppose."

"It didn't last."

"When she took my boy away, I almost went nuts. But I met Eunice, and she was great. Once I married her, Davey could come and stay with us in the summer and at holidays. That was good for a while, but Eunice didn't like me being gone all the time. She took up with the local veterinarian, if you can believe that."

"Wow." I didn't want to know more about Del's personal tragedies, but he was on a roll. "After Eunice I moved in with Ilene. I didn't intend to get married again, but when she got pregnant for Cassidy, she insisted we needed to make it legal, so I did." He leaned toward me, his eyes angry. "Three years later she tells me Cassidy isn't my kid anyway, and she's leaving me to be with the girl's real father."

What do you say when a guy tells you something like that? "That must have been tough."

He shrugged. "She's a spoiled brat anyway. Grew up to be exactly like her mother."

By this time I'd concluded I was going to hear the whole story, so I asked, "You tried marriage one more time?"

"Yeah. Would you believe it was another Eunice? I mean, how many women named Eunice does a guy even meet, much less marry two of them?"

"What happened with her?"

"Boredom," he replied. "The band broke up, and I gave up music. I started working at a cement plant, which meant I had to come home to the same woman, the same stories, every single night. When I couldn't stand it anymore, I told her I was out of there."

"And you don't plan to marry again."

He waved the idea of it away. "I pick up a lady, stay with her until I get tired, and then move on."

Except Shawna got tired of you first, I thought. Del seemed to recall that same thing, because he mumbled something about getting pancakes before they were all gone.

When I told Julie about the conversation later, she frowned. "Don't they say rapists are often trying to dominate women to make up for some lack they feel in themselves?"

"Del seems to like the seduction part of a relationship. And I have to say he doesn't seem like the type to use violence to get what he wants."

"Maybe," Julie replied, "but I'm going to keep him in the Maybe column, no matter what he says about rushing to the delivery room to be with Wife Number One."

Chapter Forty-Two

Earl (Earl & Wilma) Thursday, 10:00 a.m./4 p.m.

Ron and I had some time to talk on the golf course while we waited for Kevin to either find his ball or admit he never would. Tommy and Dean helped him look along the reedy edge of a pond. I stood next to the cart and waited, a little disgusted. I hate making the golfers behind us wait, but Kevin doesn't seem to mind at all.

Ron was the designated cart-driver, since he's not allowed to play yet. We talked about the interviews we'd done and, reminded of what Wilma had told me about Hank, I passed it on.

"I've been wondering about Hank too," Ron said when I finished. "I could have sworn he mentioned driving a semi in the past, but when I asked him about it, he claimed he never has."

"Wilma said he used the words 'six days on the road,' like in that song about trucking."

Ron rubbed his forehead, trying to bring up a memory. "I remember somebody telling how loud it was in the cabs back then, and how it was blazing hot in summer and freezing cold in winter." Ron scrunched up his face. "Hank's face comes to my mind." He shook the idea out of his head. "Maybe he was standing around when someone else said it, and I got them mixed up."

It struck me that we all dismissed Hank easily, maybe too easily, because he's a good guy in a sad situation. That left me thinking, so when we got home from the links, I hung around outside until Hank rode by on his bike. "How's it going?" I called out.

"It's going." He coasted to a stop. "Can't ask for more than that."

I'd tried to come up with a way to open a conversation about the past, and I admit the result was clumsy. "Wilma and me were talking about that project Julie's got going." When Hank didn't answer I said, "Were you and Janis married in July of '67?"

Hank's lips pulled in and his voice turned shaky, like he was either mad or scared. "What are you all up to, Earl? Why'd Julie pick that date to ask everybody about?"

I can't lie to a person's face, so I told the truth. "The law is looking for a man who was at a certain place on a certain night in Nashville. I think that man might be you."

He wanted to deny it, but he couldn't make the words come out. Instead he asked, "You were in the military, right, Earl?"

I stepped closer so we could talk without being overheard. "Navy."

"I was army—for about two months." Sitting back on his bike seat, Hank lit a cigarette. When he'd taken the first drag, he went on. "I did basic training at Fort Bragg, and I hated every minute of it. Someone was always in my face, hollering at me to do it better and faster. They say they break you down to build you back up again, but all I felt was the breaking-down part."

"I hear that." It had been hard on me too, a farm boy who'd never been away from home before. Until then, nobody had ever called me an idiot, not even a coach, since playing sports had been impossible for a kid needed on the family farm. My time at the Great Lakes Training Center was a real eye-opener, but I'd made it through by reminding myself that everyone got the same treatment. If they could live through it, so could I.

Taking another drag, Hank went on. "After basic they told me I'd be sent to Fort Benning for more training, what they called AIT. Scuttlebutt said that from there we'd head to Vietnam, this little country most of us couldn't have found on a map. All of a sudden it was in the news every day, and what I heard made me sick. A couple of the guys knew boys who got killed over there. Others came back so weird they were scary. Word was they'd been through hell."

I saw where his story was heading. "You decided to desert."

Hank made an angry gesture. "I didn't decide anything. They gave me leave, so I went home to Arizona. When it came time to go back, I—I couldn't make myself do it."

"What did you do?"

He sighed. "I got drunk for three days. I'm not sure how I avoided the MPs, but I woke up in a hotel room, hung over and AWOL. I called home; my mom was hysterical. She said I should leave the country. Then Dad got on the phone and said I had to turn myself in. I didn't want to do either of those things."

"So you got yourself a new identity."

"Yeah. My granddad was in this care facility, and a guy in the other bed, who was about my age, had been in a bad car accident and was in a coma. I'd noticed his wallet in the drawer of the bedside table when a nurse opened it." He shrugged. "I don't know how the plan came into my head, but it did. I went in, said goodbye to Grandpa, and stole the wallet. Neither of them even knew I was there."

"What about your parents?"

"I wrote them a note and put it in Grandpa's Bible. He wasn't going to live long, so I figured they'd find it in a week or so." Hank's bulldog face sagged even farther. "I never got over feeling bad about being such a disappointment to them."

"They probably understood."

His head hung lower. "Maybe, but it's got to be hard to have a son that's a coward."

Though I didn't like that word, it's what most of the vets I knew would call him. Desertion is hard to understand for guys who went and did what our country asked us to do. We didn't want to leave our homes and families to get shot at neither, but we figured it was part of being a citizen. They talk now about the whole thing being for oil company profits, but for us it was about doing what Uncle Sam asked. While I understand someone being a Conscientious Objector or even running off to Canada, I won't lie and say I approve of it.

Rather than comment on Hank's decision, I took the conversation a different way. "What did you do when you left Arizona?"

He chuckled grimly. "I was lost at first. I'd spent my whole life in Flagstaff, except for the eight weeks of basic training, and I wasn't even sure what the state after New Mexico was. I started hitching rides. I got picked up in Nebraska by a trucker who said his outfit always needed drivers. My dad ran an excavating business, so I could handle about any kind of vehicle. I went and signed up."

"As the patient from the hospital."

"They didn't care who I was once I said I could drive a truck and I didn't mind long hauls. Me and Greg were similar in coloring and both pretty skinny, and I let my hair and beard grow out to change my looks. After some training, a CDL test, and a couple weeks of riding with an experienced driver, I started trucking all over the Midwest. Six months later I stopped to eat and met this waitress, Kelly. She was something."

That I could relate to. “First time I saw Wilma, I said, ‘That’s the girl for me.’”

“That’s how it was for me too, at least at first.” He smiled at the memory. “I asked her out about six times before she finally said yes, but after that, whenever I was close, I’d take a few hours to be with her. We went to the movies. I took her to some kind of fair in June.” His eyes went soft. “We’d walk around the city and talk about stuff.”

“You didn’t tell her the truth about who you were.”

“No.” Hank crushed out his cigarette and dropped the butt into a can he’d wired to his handlebars. “I said I was from New Mexico and got rated 4F because of foot problems.” He let out a breath and a cloud of smoke. “The truest thing I said was that I was crazy about her.”

“You planned to settle in Nashville.”

“Yeah. I gave my boss at the trucking firm notice and started looking for a new job and a place for us to live. We talked about staying in her apartment, but the landlord was a jerk. She suspected he went into her place while she was at work, because she’d find her underwear drawer all messed up. He had all these rules too, like no male visitors.” Hank’s cheeks flushed. “We did our thing in a park down the road.”

“That’s why the cops didn’t find your prints at her place.”

He chuckled. “In the long run, the guy’s stupid rule was good. They never figured out that Greg Miles was actually Michael D. Richfield, U.S. Army AWOL.”

“Tell me about the murders.”

Hank bit his lip. “I got to Kelly’s around ten-fifteen that night. Her shift ended at ten, and she rode the bus home, so it was usually ten-thirty by the time she got there. I sat on a bench and kind of snoozed until some odd sounds woke me. At first, I couldn't tell where they came from."

"What did you hear?"

"A fight. Following the sound, I went up to the apartment below Kelly's. In the window I saw two men going at it hammer and tongs. I ran to the door and banged on it a few times, but they didn't stop. The door was locked, so I finally kicked it in. I hollered, 'Stop, or I'll call the police.'"

"Did you know the people who lived there?"

Hank shook his head. "Kelly had told me it was a couple, and the guy worked nights. She tried to be quiet during the day, because that's when he had to sleep."

"What happened when you got in there?"

Hank's gaze unfocused as his memory returned to the scene he'd witnessed. "The woman was sprawled on the couch, her chest all bloody and her eyes wide open. The place had gone quiet, and I didn't see either man. I went over to the woman and felt for a pulse, but she was dead. Then I heard a noise at the back of the apartment. I tiptoed back there, scared half to death I was going to get jumped. A sliding door that opened onto the back yard was open, and I saw a man climbing over the fence."

"You didn't chase him?"

"I was going to, but then I heard a moan behind me. I turned and found a man—the husband, I learned later— slumped against the wall in the kitchen." Hank shuddered. "He'd been stabbed, like his wife."

"Geez."

Hank stared at the horizon over my shoulder. "I didn't know what to do, Earl. I laid the guy down flat, thinking maybe he wouldn't bleed so much that way. That's how I got blood on my shirt. He opened his eyes once, and I told him to hang on and I'd get help. Their phone was mounted on the wall overhead, and I started to reach for it." Meeting my gaze Hank confessed, "I gotta admit, I hesitated. If I called, I knew the cops would ask me questions I didn't want to answer. I'd probably get fingerprinted, and they'd find out I wasn't Greg Miles. That meant arrest, trial, separation from Kelly, the end of everything."

"What did you do?"

"I made the call." He stretched out a hand, palm up. "I had to." His expression turned rueful. "About the time they answered, the guy made a weird sound, and I realized he'd died." He cleared his throat. "I gave them the address and hung up."

"Then you ran away."

He nodded. "I'd only touched the phone and the doorknob, so I wiped them down with my handkerchief. I figured I'd leave and then come back later, like I'd just arrived." He paused, his expression grim. "But when I stepped out the door, this guy was coming up the walk, and he hollered, "What are you doing in there?" I panicked. I barreled past him and ran. Behind me, he started shouting, 'Stop! Stop!' And in the background, I heard sirens."

"You kept running."

"Not far enough." He rubbed his forehead. "I did the dumbest thing. I waited for Kelly at the bus stop. I told her there'd been trouble and I had to go away for a while, but I'd send for her when I could."

"What did she say?"

"She was okay until she noticed the blood on my shirt." Hank's eyes met mine. "Earl, you should have seen her face. She said, 'Greg, what did you do?' The sirens shut down all of a sudden, like somebody turned off a radio. Everything got quiet, but I saw the flashing lights behind me reflecting off Kelly's glasses. She asked again what had happened, and I heard a cop call out to another cop to start a search. I backed away from her, turned around, and ran off like a madman."

I took in a long breath. "You're telling me you didn't hurt those people."

"As God is my witness, Earl, I tried to help. I was too late."

"And the guy who went out the back?"

"Only saw his backside disappearing over the fence. Blue jeans and black shoes."

"Not much to go on."

"Nope. I was a way better prospect for the cops to arrest."

"Where'd you go?"

Hank sighed. "I hitched to Arkansas, got work there, and kept my head down. *Miles* is a common name, and I told people I went by the middle name on the license, which was Henry. Next job I took it a step farther, Hank. After a few years I applied to legally change my last name to Edmonds. Told the judge my dad had been abusive, and I wanted a new name to start married life."

"You'd met a girl."

"Janis." At the mention of his wife's name, Hank's face softened. "I was sure I'd never fall in love again, but she was something else."

"And Kelly?"

"From what I read in the papers, she believed what everybody else did: I went after the wife, killed her when she resisted me, and stabbed her husband when he came to her rescue."

"They never caught the real killer?"

"Why would they? They were looking for me."

Maybe I'm naïve, but it sounded like the truth, at least in terms of what I knew of Hank. "What do you think happened?"

"I think it went exactly like they said, but with the guy I saw go out the back. He got away with it because I showed up at exactly the wrong time." He shook his head. "The killer must have loved the part where I didn't stick around to defend myself."

Chapter Forty-Three

Tommy (Tommy & Alice) Thursday, 6:00 p.m.

Earl called a meeting for just the guys in the activity room Thursday evening, supposedly to discuss park rules. Ron and I walked over, and Earl brought Al in the golf cart. It felt cloak-and-dagger-ish, but Earl insisted we had to talk without the girls. After he relayed Hank's confession, we were silent for a while. Though the sixties are long gone, once in a while they reach out and grab you by the throat. It was a strange time: Many were thrilled to receive a 4F or 2S deferment from military service, but nobody wanted to be known as a draft-dodger who didn't go when his number came up.

Now somebody we knew was that guy. All these years later, I wasn't sure how I felt about it.

"We can't tell the women." Al, who is probably Hank's best friend in the park, was vehement.

"We have to," Earl argued. "It proves Hank didn't kill anybody."

"It doesn't prove anything," Ron countered. "All you've got is a story he told you."

"Who'd make up something like that?" Earl was right. It wasn't exactly something a guy would invent to make himself look better.

"If we tell the girls, they'll pass it on to O'Connor," Al said. "Hank could go to prison."

"After all this time?"

"Guys go AWOL these days because they don't want to be sent to places like Afghanistan. The military doesn't want it to look like it's okay to leave if you don't like the assignment."

"Al's right. Punishing deserters, even years later, is considered a deterrent for others who might consider it." I gave a quick recap of the law. "There are three possible charges—absence without leave, known as AWOL, desertion, and missing movement. Missing movement is charged when a service member doesn't board a ship or aircraft, either intentionally or out of neglect. AWOL becomes desertion after thirty days. Hank is guilty of all three. It's up to the tribunal that hears his case, but they tend to take a hard stance. There are serious penalties, up to and including death."

Earl's eyes went wide. "You don't think Hank would be executed."

I shook my head. "That hasn't happened since World War II, but he could do prison time if some gung-ho officer gets assigned his case."

There was another silence as we all considered that. "Could we tell O'Connor we're sure no one here at B-Bird killed those people?"

"Why would he take our word? The story would have to come out."

After yet another silence, Ron said, "Let's give it a couple of days. Maybe we can think of how to do this without messing up Hank's life."

"All right," I said. "Then we agree we won't tell our wives until we decide on it together."

"Agreed," Ron and Al said. Earl took longer, and his yes, when it finally came, was conspicuously reluctant.

Chapter Forty-Four

Alice (Tommy & Alice) Friday, 9:30 a.m.

I'm aware that it's crazy to interfere in the relationships of others, but Ray O'Connor was obviously clueless when it came to love. A man over thirty who's still on his own has probably sabotaged a string of promising affairs by not recognizing the unspoken—yet very real—rules of the romance game in this day and age. In the past, the promise of sex led men to commit to a woman long-term. Now that sex is easy and everywhere, some men view dating as a way of life. Marlene might or might not be O'Connor's ideal partner, but in my estimation, she'd never garner the nerve to ask him what his intentions for their future were. As for the detective, I pegged him as the type who'd couldn't fathom that he might lose a woman he cared about until she was gone.

When I saw the man's car at Julie's Friday morning, I made a decision. Picking up a coffee cake I'd made for Tommy and me to have at our mid-morning break, I hurried across the street.

I knocked, and Julie called for me to come in. O'Connor was sitting at the table and Julie was pouring them each an iced tea. "How about a slice of this to go with your drinks?" I invited, and O'Connor perked up like a seal offered a fish.

Since it had been a while since we met, Julie said, "Detective, you'll remember my friend Alice Murgasson. She's helping with our project."

"Oh, yes," he said politely, but his eye was on the treat. Taking it from me, Julie cut the detective a hefty chunk. Hers was much smaller, and I said I'd wait and have some later with Tommy. The detective remembered my husband and asked about him. I said he was fine and turned to my purpose.

"I can't stay," I told Julie, "but I wanted to let you know my nephew from Charleston will be here this afternoon. You said you might be able to fix him up with Marlene in the office, right?" Julie gave me a look, but I went right on. "I think they'd be perfect for each other, and you said she isn't seeing anyone seriously."

Julie glanced at O'Connor, who'd stopped with a forkful of cake halfway to his mouth. "Actually, Marlene is seeing someone."

"But she isn't engaged or anything, right?" Turning to O'Connor I explained, "Kevin's a real sweetheart. He'll be taking the bar exam soon, I know he and Marlene will hit it off." I rose from the chair. "If he arrives before closing, I'd like you to take him down to the office and introduce them." Picking up the remains of the coffee cake I said, "It was good seeing you again, Detective."

When I glanced back, O'Connor was looking dazed and a little unhappy. Julie raised an eyebrow as if to say, *You sly devil.*

I winked. I'd given him a shove. Now we'd see what happened.

Chapter Forty-Five

Earl (Earl & Wilma) Friday, 1:00 p.m.

The subject of Hank Edmonds' confession weighed on my mind. The guys had agreed to keep it from the girls, but Wilma had been honest about Del's rotten behavior. She'd said it wasn't right for husbands and wives to keep secrets, which meant I had to be honest. Though I felt bad going against what us guys had agreed on, I told her the whole thing.

"What are you going to say to Julie?" she asked.

"The other guys don't want to tell the women anything."

Wilma frowned. "They said we'd help the police find a killer. Now that we know what happened, why keep it a secret?"

"They want to figure out a way to handle things so it isn't too hard on Hank."

"But how can they justify that if Hank's really Greg Miles?"

I was torn between loyalty to the guys and Wilma's doubt. "It's like when you girls did that song for the Christmas Follies. You didn't lie to us about what you were doing, but you didn't tell us everything."

She gave me a look. "This is more serious than a silly song, Earl."

She had me there.

Whenever I have a question to wrestle with, I take a walk.

Shrinks have all kinds of analysis on why walking helps with thinking. I don't know about that. I only know it does. You look up at the sky or out at the land or even down at your feet, going in and out, and somehow things fall into place. The importance of some things settles in. The unimportant things fade. The question of which is which gets clearer. And if you're lucky, the answer becomes obvious.

I walked the road that edges the park, Main Street, which is divided into directions: Main East, then South, then West, and then North. That took me to the park entrance. If I'd taken Main East again, I'd have returned home, but since I needed more thinking time, I turned left and took the street that leads out to the highway. B-Bird Avenue is a half mile of skinny road with not much along its edges, since it runs through an area that's pretty swampy. That might sound bad, but it's why B-Bird isn't shoulder to shoulder with a Walmart or a strip of hair salons and tattoo parlors. At its other end, Ambler Road is six lanes of almost constant traffic.

As I neared the highway, I saw that a snazzy little vintage Corvette had turned onto B-Bird Avenue and parked half-on and half-off the road. Alongside it was the driver, an attractive female wearing those pants that look like tights and a long, flowy shirt over top. Long, blond hair hid her face as she stood with her fists on her hips, looking into the machinery under the car's raised hood with a puzzled expression.

"Having car trouble?"

My question brought a jump and a gasp. As she turned toward me, I saw drawn-on eyebrows and bright, red lips that formed a circle of surprise. "Sorry." I stopped and raised my hands, palms out. "I'm out walking, and I saw you looking…well, confused."

Whatever apprehension my arrival had caused seemed to evaporate. "I was coming down Ambler and the engine suddenly cut out. I had just enough momentum to turn in here and get out of the traffic." A head shake emphasized the next words. "No idea what's wrong. I'm an idiot when it comes to cars."

"I'm no mechanic, but I can take a look if you like."

"Please."

Working on a farm, you get to know a little about engines, not modern ones so much, but this one was from the days when I studied Chilton's Motor Manual like it was a textbook. Peering under the hood, I noticed wet spots. "Did you wash this thing recently?"

"I did."

"Under the hood too?"

"Yes. Someone told me it's good to do that once in a while."

"True. But if the distributor cap gets water in it, a car can stall out."

"Oh."

I unhooked the connections and took a look. "Yep. There's your problem, I bet." Using my handkerchief, I dried the cap off. "Let's give it a minute to dry, and then we'll try it."

"Thanks, um…"

"Name's Earl."

"Thank you, Earl. I'm Kim."

"Nice to meet you."

"I'm lucky you came along." Kim took out a phone and glanced at the screen. "I have exactly fourteen minutes to get to the club where I'm performing or I'll be in trouble…again." A smile and a little shrug said that wasn't a big worry.

"You're a singer?"

"Yeah, sort of. I do impersonations of famous singers."

"Oh."

Pride overtook modestly and Kim said, "I'm best known for my Katy Perry, but I also do Taylor Swift, Cher, Adele, Ariana Grande, and Streisand." She leaned toward me. "Everyone does Streisand."

"Wow. That's a lot."

A nod accepted that as praise, though to be honest I had no idea who most of those women were. I know Cher and Barbra, of course. The rest were only names I've heard on TV.

"I should give you a ticket, so you can come to the show."

"You don't need to—"

"It's not a big deal." Kim paused. "Are you married, Earl?"

"Yeah. Wilma's my wife."

"Great. We'll make it two." Taking a little pink notebook with a matching pen from the glovebox, Kim spoke the words aloud. "*Allow two people into any show at no cost.* It's the Silver Bullet on 54. I'll be there until the middle of February. I'll put my phone number on here too, in case there's a problem with the bouncer. He can be grumpy sometimes, so give me a call if he won't honor this." Holding out the paper until I took it, Kim said, "Really, you should come."

"Thanks, but we don't even know if I fixed your car yet."

"I appreciate the effort, either way." The under-the-eyelashes look that came my way made me kind of nervous, so I stuck the paper in my pocket and said, "Let's try it."

The car started right up, and Kim clapped enthusiastically. "Thanks again, Earl." Checking the rear view mirror and waiting for a car to pass, Kim did a U-ey and drove off, tooting the horn as a final goodbye.

When I got to the park entrance, the car that had passed was parked at the office. Del Hanna had climbed out, and he flagged me down. "Who was the good-looking woman you were talking to, Earl?"

For a second I bit my tongue, unable to believe he had the nerve to speak to me after putting his slimy moves on my wife. After a few seconds I made a conscious effort to relax my shoulders. I'd promised Wilma I wouldn't make trouble, and, judging by his open gaze, Del thought Wilma hadn't told me what he'd done.

"Um, that was Kim. I was able to help with some car trouble."

He ignored my cold tone. "A knight in shining armor, eh?"

I shrugged. "It wasn't a big deal."

"And what did you get out of it? I saw her give you something."

"Kim's got a night club act, I guess. Wilma and me are invited to go there some night and see the show."

He was definitely interested. "Really. Are you going to go?"

"Probably not. We don't go out much at night."

Del's manner turned even oilier. "I'd like to see the show. If you're not going to use that pass, I'll take it."

The guy's nerve was unbelievable, but it didn't matter to me one way or the other. I took out the paper and handed it over.

His smile got even bigger. "She included her phone number. Do you think if I called her, she'd have a drink with me after the show?"

"Um—"

He interrupted what I might have said with another oily grin. "It can't hurt to ask, right?"

I thought about it for a second. Kim had seemed to me someone who could handle a guy like Del, no problem. "You're both adults," I told him. "What you do is up to you."

Later that day, Ron stopped by to borrow my band saw. While we were in the shed, he told me Del was spreading the word that he'd talked me into giving him access to a really hot nightclub singer. "I suppose you weren't interested in going to the show," Ron said, "but why would you give any woman's number to Del Hanna?"

"Kim isn't a woman."

Ron's chin backed right into his neck. "Are you saying she's a he?"

"I never understood why a bull wants to dress up like a heifer," I told him, "but I sure as heck can tell the difference between the two."

Chapter Forty-Six

Julie (Ron & Julie) Friday, 2:00 p.m.

Wilma is amazing. What would have been a plain, black-and-white monstrosity in my hands was becoming a work of art, with beautiful edging she conjured with something called sparkle yarn, which I didn't even know existed. She'd suggested using metallic embroidery thread rather than yarn to lead from the labels to the map locations, which looked better and took up less space. She also managed to hide the ends of the thread much more effectively than I'd have done, so the result looked finished and professional.

Alice had done more than her share of typing information onto the label templates. In order to cut down on the number of labels we had on the board, we put one household on each. Ours looked like this:

Ron and Julie Rogers
Egret Street, Lot 10
Marisette, Wisconsin

Alice and Tommy's looked like this:

Tommy and Alice Murgasson
Egret Street, Lot 9
Tommy: Phu Bai, Vietnam. Alice: Bradenton, FL

I even called my friend Cheri up in Quebec for her information, so she wouldn't be left out. Hers looked like this:

Cheri Armand

Bittern Street, Lot 16
Stratford, ONT, Canada

As we finished each page I printed it off, separated the labels, and plotted how they'd be arranged. We wanted it to be easy to find a particular person, so I alphabetized them by last name. Alice pointed out that residents often don't know each other's last names, but again Wilma had a brilliant idea. She dug up an extra park directory, and in a stroke of genius, asked Jessica LaTran to cut out the photos of each resident and glue them next to the labels.

"How did you get her to do that?" I asked.

Wilma shrugged. "You said she got upset about not getting to do all the interviews. Some people like doing one thing and doing it well, so I gave her that."

"Wilma Schmidt, you are a very wise woman," I told her.

As Karen hounded our volunteers into getting their assigned tasks done, she confided that Jessica had been right (not that I would admit that to her). While most who'd volunteered to help were Johnny-on-the-Spot, a few became lackadaisical after a day or so. If the weather was nice, they put off information gathering to do something fun. If the weather wasn't nice, they didn't feel like going out to knock on doors. Like a stern grandmother, Karen urged them to do as they'd promised, establishing firm expectations and making our appreciation known when the job was done.

Between the display and my last few interviews, I was exhausted when the Silver Sleuths met at Tommy's that afternoon to discuss our findings. I started things off, explaining that I'd proven, as far as I could manage, that fifteen of the men on my list were not Greg Miles. Ron went next, saying he considered everyone on his list to be unlikely. Tommy said the same, adding his opinion that mistakes had been made up in Nashville. "The woman who wrote that note is wrong. I don't think the guy is here."

"Me neither," Al chimed in. Karen had been looking at the master list, but her head rose as he spoke, and I saw surprise on her face. The way he said it, and the way Earl agreed a little too quickly, was suspicious. Alice's frown said she'd drawn the same conclusion. Wilma seemed interested in something across the street, though it was only Harry power-washing his carport. I couldn't tell if she was even listening as Earl gave his report. "Wilma and me talked to everyone on our lists, and we haven't got anything to tell Detective O'Connor."

"We should go over the names anyway," I urged. "One of us might spot something that was missed."

"That Terry Bidwell sounds like a possibility to me," Al said. "Anybody with a wife that watches him like she does has probably done something that makes her distrust him."

"Alice and I checked his story out," I said. "He sold vacuum cleaners door-to-door for a couple of years, though he doesn't like admitting it. His territory was way south of Nashville."

Al shifted his chair. "Doesn't mean he didn't go other places."

His argument was weak, but I dutifully made a note that Bidwell's story needed further corroboration. "He fits the description, medium height, blue eyes."

"That description is pretty vague," Tommy said. "What's middle height? A lot of tall people get shorter as our joints settle, and eye color is changeable these days with contacts."

The other men nodded, and I sensed rebellion in the ranks. Ignoring them, I read a few more names. Alice and Karen tried to keep an open discussion going, but everyone else seemed ready to dismiss the whole idea of us finding Greg Miles.

"Who do we think we are, playing detective?" Tommy asked. "If someone lies, how would we know?"

He was right, of course, but I went on to the next name, keeping my arguments inside my head.

Even Ron turned traitor. "We aren't accomplishing anything."

I tried not to show that I was hurt by that. "O'Connor thinks it's worth doing. He came to us."

"He's going through the motions," Tommy argued. "He wants to report to the Nashville police that he looked into the possibility of Miles living at B-Bird."

I glanced at Alice, who gave me a tiny head shake to indicate she didn't get it either. Where had this sudden resistance come from?

Taking a second to quell my frustration I said, "All right. Let's finish going through the list this last time, and then I'll tell O'Connor we did what we could." Sensing relief from the men, I added, "If this is it, we need to focus, so we hand over the best information we can get."

No one objected, so I continued down the list. "Arden Benson."

Karen spoke up. "He was in Texas from '65 to '71. He's got some interesting stories about being a roughneck."

"Any proof?"

"When I said I was interested, he went inside and got a photo of himself standing next to a big oil derrick. The date on the margin said it was from August of 1967."

"So he could have been in Nashville in July," Al said.

"I'm not sure how he'd have held down two jobs at once."

Al merely sniffed, so I went on. "Hank Edmonds?"

Silence. Finally Earl said, "He told Wilma he lived in Little Rock in 1967."

I looked to Wilma. "Any proof?"

She shook her head, but Tommy said, "Didn't you say that's where Janis grew up, Wilma?" That got a nod. "I've heard Hank tell about them meeting at a factory where they both worked."

"But we don't know when he started, or where he was before he hired on there," Alice said.

"We're becoming invasive, like the KGB or something." It was the first time I'd ever seen Tommy react with irritation toward his wife, and it made me hesitate.

It was true. We were questioning everything we knew about people we liked. Was this what it was like to be a cop? Trusting nobody? Assuming everyone lied when it suited them?

On the other hand, someone at B-Bird was wanted in the deaths of two innocent people. Even if it was snoopy, I wanted to learn who that person was. I wanted him brought to justice. I wanted to believe we'd succeed through organization, persistence, or even blind luck.

Shortly after that, the meeting broke up. My mood was somewhere between anger and despair. The enthusiasm we'd begun with was clearly dead. What had happened?

Wilma and Earl went off with the briefest of goodbyes, looking faintly guilty. Tommy and Ron stood side by side, presenting a united front. Al wouldn't meet my eyes.

"Want to go for a walk before dinner?" Alice asked Karen and me. “We can burn off some calories before we load up again.”

“I’ll drive Al home,” Ron offered. As they climbed into the golf cart, they both looked faintly guilty too. Tommy busied himself with cleaning up the cups and napkins we’d left behind.

As soon as we were away from the guys, Alice said, “Okay, what was that?”

Karen shook her head. “I have no idea, but it was weird.”

“I think Wilma knows something,” I said. “She kind of ignored the whole thing, like she wanted to pretend it wasn’t happening.”

Alice’s brow rose. “If she’s got a secret, I’ll find out what it is.”

Karen snickered. “How? Are you going to tear out her fingernails?”

“Silence is Wilma’s only defense,” Alice replied. “Once I get her alone and start her talking, she’ll tell me everything she knows.”

Chapter Forty-Seven

Karen (Al & Karen) Thursday, 4:00 p.m.

I hadn't seen Marlene for a few days, so I peeled away from Alice and Julie to stop at the office. It was closing time, but she shot me a raised-brow look that signaled she had something to tell me. Taking a seat, I paged through an old magazine while she dealt with questions and complaints from various residents. I wondered how many of them were here every day, or at least several times a week, to ask questions and air grievances. In many cases it was probably a case of wanting someone to listen to their concerns. Marlene was a patient woman, and I guessed that quality was important in her job.

A tiny woman I'd seen around the park approached the desk, checkbook in hand. "I need to pay my rent."

"You don't have to, Mrs. Dunn. Your rent is already paid."

I saw her only in profile, but I read irritation in her posture. "There's no check stub here in my book."

"We set up automatic withdrawals, remember? You, um, you forgot to pay a few times, and I suggested we could withdraw the money out of your bank account every month. That way you don't have to worry about it anymore."

"You take the money?"

"Yes."

"Out of my account."

Marlene cleared her throat. "You signed a form so we can do that."

"I would never let someone take my money without my say-so."

"You wanted it that way, so you don't have to remember to pay it."

Her white head shook, and I heard a sound of disgust. "What's to stop you from taking money from me to buy yourself something nice?"

"We wouldn't do that."

"But what's to stop you?"

Marlene paused, and I imagined what she might say: Ethics. Rules. Decency. Fear of prison.

Instead she said, "Dan said this was the best way."

The woman's manner did a one-eighty. "Danny said that?"

"Yes." Digging in a file cabinet, Marlene found a single sheet of paper. "Here's the agreement."

Mrs. Dunn read it over and touched the signature lovingly. "My boy looks out for me," she said. "He's busy at work—vice president at his company, you know—but he takes care of his mother." She picked up her checkbook and put the pen back into the mug on the counter. "So I don't need to pay the rent? Danny's taken care of it?"

"He has. Enjoy the rest of your day."

As she left, Marlene shot me a look of amusement, and I wondered if the scene I'd witnessed was repeated monthly. When the office cleared out, Marlene asked me to lock the door and turn the sign to "Closed" while she put things away. "Ray's taking me out to dinner tonight," she announced. "He says we have things to discuss."

"What things would those be?"

"He wasn't specific, but he did ask how far away I'm willing to live from work."

"And you said…?"

Her cheeks turned pink. "I didn't know what to say. Do you think he meant we might move in together?"

"I thought you'd talked about it already."

She sighed. "When I kind of hinted we should, he didn't say no, but he changed the subject pretty quickly." Marlene's dark eyes widened. "I've been afraid to mention it again, but now Boom! Out of the blue he wants to talk about our future."

"Something must have given him a push." I picked up my phone and keys. "The funny thing with men is, you might never figure out where that push came from."

Chapter Forty-Eight

Julie (Ron & Julie) Friday 6:00 p.m./Saturday, 9:00 a.m.

Friday evening, four of us tried out a new restaurant on the coast, Captain Nan's. We went for the Early Bird Special, which Ron jokes is offered because old people can't stay awake for dinner at eight. Tommy volunteered to drive, and Alice and I chatted amiably in the back seat as we traveled down Highway 19. When we arrived, Tommy immediately excused himself to go to the restroom (I suspect prostate trouble). Once he was gone, Alice said to Ron, "I hear you guys know which man at B-Bird is Greg Miles."

Ron glanced toward the bathroom as if seeking help. "Um…it's a theory. Nothing solid."

Alice's gaze speared him like a bug on a pin. "And you don't want to share it with us why?"

He rearranged his silverware before answering. "No sense ruining a man's reputation on rumor."

"Rumor. Then it's something you heard from a third party?"

Ron grabbed at the lifeline she'd tossed him. "Yeah. A third party." I knew Alice well enough to realize she was merely giving my husband enough rope to hang himself.

When Tommy returned Alice said, "Ron was telling us about the clue you got from…" Pausing, she turned to Ron. "Who did you say the story came from?"

The best my husband could do was an "Um" and a pleading glance at Tommy. Better equipped to deal with his wife's directness, Tommy said, "Earl heard a story. We're in the process of figuring out how much truth there is to it."

Alice glanced at me triumphantly. She'd gotten the guys to admit there was information, and we now knew it had come from Earl. I guessed she'd be hunting Wilma down tomorrow for an interrogation.

I'd intended to worm answers out of Ron once we were back home, but the end of our evening banished thoughts of that. When he turned the key in the lock, Ron frowned. "It's open," he said. "I must have forgotten to lock up."

That was unusual, but we all forget things from time to time. Once we were inside he asked, "Did you leave a light on in the bathroom?"

I peered down the hallway. "I don't think so."

A feeling I've read about but had never experienced followed: the sense of violation that comes when you realize someone has been in your house uninvited. We reacted like mad people, turning on every light in the place and searching frantically for signs of theft.

Everything was where we'd left it. Nothing was missing.

In the end we looked at each other and grinned. "You forgot the light. I forgot to lock up," Ron said. "We're sliding into old age."

The next morning I stopped at Karen's to tell her what Alice had made the guys admit to. Al was in his usual spot on the porch, and sensing I had secrets to tell, Karen invited, "Come in. I made cinnamon rolls."

As we sat at the dining table, munching on the warm, sticky

buns and sipping coffee, I told Karen Earl had uncovered the identity of the man posing as Greg Miles. "He'd have been the last one of us I'd have guessed would figure it out, she said."

"It's nice that our efforts paid off, but I wish we knew what they know."

"I asked Al, but he won't talk about it." She wiped her fingers on a napkin. "Who would they be protecting?"

We listed men our husbands would feel they had to shelter from criminal prosecution. There weren't many, since, as Karen pointed out, murder charges are pretty serious.

"They wouldn't go out of their way to protect Del or Matthew or Ty Shaw. I mean, I like Ty all right, but Al says he's full of himself."

I took out my phone and scrolled through the master list. "Could it be someone we haven't interviewed yet?"

"Or someone one of them interviewed. Earl's list is most likely."

We perused the names Earl had originally been assigned. He'd found them all unlikely, and I had to agree.

"Maybe it was someone on Wilma's list," Karen suggested. "They were working together."

Switching to Wilma's list, I shared the view of my screen with Karen. After some discussion we starred Wilma and Earl's neighbor, Don Burrows, who'd listed Clarksville, TN, as his home in 1967. "It's close to Nashville," Karen said. We also included our Sunday Services organizer, who'd been an itinerant preacher in Tennessee at the time. Karen suggested we include Hank Edmonds. "Wilma acted funny when his name came up. I happened to be looking her way, and I could swear she looked scared."

I put a star by Hank's name, but none of the three seemed like a murderer to me. As I stared at the list, a thought occurred to me. "What about people who work at the park, like George Zelli?"

"Yeah." Karen pointed at me. "He often shows up at park events, he's got kind of a loud voice, and he's the right age."

I added George's name to the master list. "It's Saturday, but I'll have Alice call and ask where he was on that date. He won't object to the council president's wife contacting him on the weekend, and she can say we want to include him on the display with everyone else."

Chapter Forty-Nine

Al (Al & Karen) Saturday, 11:30 a.m.

Hank's truck stopped outside my place on Saturday, and I figured he was on his way to feed Janis her lunch. Karen was inside, making lunch and probably throwing away perfectly edible food in the process. Hank didn't get out of the vehicle, so I got my cane and limped down the steps. When I leaned into his open window, he got right to his reason for stopping. "Earl told you about Nashville, right?"

"He did." His shoulders slumped, and I went on, "We talked about it, Earl, Tommy, Ron, and me. We don't want to make trouble for you." I saw his head bob in the slightest of nods, but he didn't say anything. "We're going to keep it to ourselves for as long as we can."

"I appreciate that, Al, but it's time I told the truth." He shivered, though it wasn't cold. "For years I've worried. When will they find me? When will it all be over? I hoped for a long time the real killer would come forward. You know, one of those death-bed confessions or like that." He turned to look at me. "I know I did things that are wrong, but I didn't kill those people. I got no way to prove it."

"It's tough, man."

"Janis needs somebody watching over her." Hank waved a hand. "She don't know I'm there, but everybody says a patient gets better attention from the staff if family stops by regular, you know? I'm not saying they aren't good people at that place, but if nobody visits and the patient doesn't know what's what, it's easy to set her somewhere and walk away."

The mental image of being pushed into a corner of a nursing home and left for hours gave me one more reason to be grateful that Karen puts up with me and all my ailments.

"Listen, Hank, you've got friends, and we're not going to leave you on your own."

"That's good to hear, Al but we both know I have to face the music, and soon." He put his hand on the gearshift. "I decided I'll turn myself in on Monday."

That set me back. "Let's talk to Tommy and Ron first," I urged. "They'll know the best way to go about it."

"What do you mean?"

"Tommy says you should talk to a lawyer before you go confessing to anything. Deals might be made in exchange for your story."

He blew out a long breath. "I'm tired, Al, tired of being scared."

"I get it." My hips were starting to burn, and I shifted my feet to ease the pain. "I'll talk to Ron today. We'll call around and see if we can get you some legal advice."

"I appreciated it, Al. It's good to have friends."

I tapped the side of his truck. "Go see your wife," I ordered. "Try not to think about Nashville for a while."

Chapter Fifty

Alice (Tommy & Alice) Saturday, 3:30 p.m.

I put in a call to George as soon as Julie suggested it. When he finally called me back it was late afternoon, since he'd been out fishing all day and had left his phone in the car for fear of losing it in the gulf. "What do you need, Alice?"

"We decided we'd like to include the staff in Julie's display. We're entering the data this weekend, so I had to disturb you on your day off."

"Not a problem," George replied. "It's nice you consider the staff part of the B-Bird family." His tone turned droll. "Marlene wasn't born in 1967, nor was our pool guy or the kid who mows. Bill lives in the park, so I'm the only one you need to hear from."

"Right. So where were you on July 7th of 1967?"

"Believe it or not, that was a night I will never forget," he replied. "I went to my first concert in Chicago: one of those on-the-lawn things where you brought your own blanket and…refreshments."

"The kind you drink or the kind you smoke?"

He chuckled. "No comment. But you'll never guess who the band was." Apparently he couldn't wait for me to even attempt it. "Does Jim Morrison ring a bell?"

"Wow. You saw The Doors in concert?"

"I've still got the ticket stub somewhere." His voice warmed with the memory. "It was wild. 'Light My Fire' was at number one on the charts. Jim was at his greatest. I had a full head of hair and all my own teeth. I count that night as the best of my early years." He sighed. "How come when you're young you don't know how good it is to be young?"

"I've got no idea, but I think it happens to everybody. I was absolutely convinced I was too skinny and my nose was too big."

"That can't be right. I'll bet guys followed you around like a pack of hounds."

And I chose the worst hound in the pack.

Aloud I said, "I was told guys got turned off because I read all the time."

"You're kidding."

"Nope." In a moment of honesty I said, "I pretty much threw my life away at seventeen."

"I'm glad you got it back. Tommy was a wreck after Ella died, but you gave him new reasons to keep going."

Thanking George, I ended the call and messaged Julie: *Grge at Doors cncert-Chicago*. That done, I checked the time. Wilma goes to the chapel on Saturday evenings, usually around six, to straighten the hymnals and reset the chairs for Sunday service. It struck me that the chapel was exactly the right atmosphere in which to find out what she was hiding. How could she lie to me in God's house?

The door was propped open to air the place, and I stopped in as if I'd been passing by and spotted her. Chatting aimlessly, I helped Wilma with her chores, moving the chairs so she could sweep and removing expired announcements from the bulletin board while she neatened the chancel and made sure there were enough chairs for the choir. As we worked, Wilma told me about a new couple who had moved in a few doors down from her and Earl. "They seem nice, and she plays the piano. I'm hoping she might give Anita a break sometimes."

"That would be nice." I didn't specify who'd benefit, but everyone would. Our pianist is ninety and half deaf, so the choir has to sing in full voice to be heard over the accompaniment.

As Wilma began putting the cleaning tools away I said, "You know something about our little project that you aren't telling."

She turned to me with a deer-in-the-headlights look. "Oh, I—I don't think—"

"Aren't we supposed to help the police solve a double murder?"

"Yes, but…" Wilma put a hand over her mouth. "When helping one person hurts another person, it's hard to decide what's right."

"It sounds like you've got a secret that's hard to keep. What if you tell me what it is, and then we'll talk about what should be done?" When she frowned I added, "I won't do anything you don't agree to. I promise."

That was all it took. A few minutes later, I knew everything Wilma knew about the night in Nashville when two people died.

Chapter Fifty-One

Julie (Ron & Julie) Saturday, 4:00 p.m.

"Ron Rogers, what is going on?" When I waved the slip of paper I'd found in his pants pocket, my husband ducked as if I'd pegged a hammer his way. Long ago, I learned to check the pockets of anything he tosses into the laundry basket, because he leaves lots of things in there, from money to extra golf tees to directions to the nearest quick-lube place. I hate ending up with soggy lumps of mystery paper at the bottom of the dryer.

"What are you planning to speak with Samuel D. Pierce, Attorney at Law, about?"

His expression said he didn't want to answer, but he did. "It's something Tommy and I are working on, Jules. I promised to keep it quiet until we have it figured out."

"Don't Alice and I deserve to know what you're up to?"

His jaw worked a little before he spoke again. "Suppose you find out something that's good but not really good. And suppose if you tell what you know, things might get bad for somebody who doesn't deserve it. What would you do?"

"If it has to do with the murders in Nashville, I'd turn it over to O'Connor. You've been telling me this whole time that our job was to find the guy. O'Connor's job is to act on the information." I pointed an accusing finger at him. "You know who it is, don't you?"

"What if Miles wasn't guilty? What if he had a different reason for running away?"

"Like I said, that's not our call."

"Sometimes you have to..." Ron stopped, unsure of how to finish.

"Have to what? Take the law into your own hands?"

"No, but—"

"Ron, do you know who here at B-Bird used to go by the name Greg Miles?"

He sighed before answering. "Yeah."

"Then you need to tell O'Connor. Today. He'll listen to the man's story and decide what should be done. You know he'll be fair."

"You're probably right," Ron admitted, "but Tommy thinks he needs legal advice before turning himself in." Ron raised a hand as if swearing himself in. "I'll call O'Connor as soon as we've talked to the lawyer. Promise."

That's when his phone rang, and all thoughts of the detective left our heads.

Chapter Fifty-Two

Karen (Al & Karen) Saturday, 4:00 p.m.

I try not to obsess about it, but I blame myself for Al's accident. I know he's not steady on his feet, and I try to watch him. The day had cooled, and without thinking, I went into the bedroom to get a sweater. Al was at the kitchen counter, putting the dishes away. I should have waited until he finished and sat down, but I was only gone a few seconds. Next thing I knew, I heard a crash and a cry of pain. I hurried out to find Al on the floor, his head spurting blood.

When scary things happen I get panicky, like anyone else. Still, Al's had so many emergencies in the last few years that I've trained myself to stop, take a breath, and think, *What do I need to do and in what order*? Three tasks came to mind. Staunch the bleeding. Assess the damage. Call for help if required.

Taking a clean dish towel from the drawer, I pressed it against the wound for a few seconds and then took a look. Along the side of Al's head was a wide gash that started bleeding again almost immediately. "Al? Can you hold this in place? I need to call the paramedics."

"Stupid," he muttered faintly. "I turned too quick. My head started spinning. The hip let go. Hit my head on the countertop going down."

"You're going to need stitches."

"Okay." He closed his eyes, and I fought back tears. He's been through so much, and now one more thing. Taking out my phone, I called 9-1-1. Once help was on the way, I called Ron. "Can you come over? Al's headed for an ambulance ride."

Ron and Julie arrived shortly after the EMTs did. I met them at the door, and we hovered out of the way as the paramedics assessed Al's condition. They asked questions from time to time, and I gave them the list: his health concerns, his medications, and his history of falls. Their expressions revealed concern that was fully justified. A multitude of factors complicate any treatment Al gets. His oxygen levels are chronically low. His lungs are a mess, as are his kidneys. Even lifting him onto a gurney was tricky, since his joints are vulnerable to injury.

Ron put an arm around me as the attendants wheeled the gurney by. The cut was bandaged, and they'd started some sort of IV. Al waved to let us know he was okay, but his smile was as weak as the one I gave in response. We followed, and when they reached the van, Ron took Al's hand and shook it as if they'd met on the street. "You behave yourself for these people, or I'll come to that hospital and beat your ass."

Al made a rude noise. "You and whose army, Peg-leg?"

That, folks, is how men say "I love you" to their friends.

Chapter Fifty-Three

Wilma (Earl & Wilma) Saturday, 6:00 p.m.

Bonnie Walston, who sits next to me in the choir, had agreed to take over my part in the duet. She didn't ask why I was backing out, which was a relief. I promised to drop off the music to her Saturday evening so she could run through it on her own before she and Del practiced after church on Sunday. I considered warning her that he was looking for a new "lady," but Bonnie is nobody's fool. She's also big enough to pound him to a powder if he tries anything with her.

Earl had received a call that morning asking if he'd sub in an afternoon foursome, and I encouraged him to go. As he packed up his golf bag, he'd cautioned me about getting home before dark, fretting because he wouldn't be back by then. I assured him I'd have plenty of time to do what I had to do and get home while it was still daylight, but by the time I straightened the chapel, talked to Alice, took the music to Bonnie, and started for home, it was getting darker by the moment. I went home by way of Osprey Street, because I enjoy seeing what Dina Canton has done to decorate her trailer. From England by way of Canada, she always has what she calls fairy lights strung outside. I'd call them Christmas lights, but these days you can buy them in colors and shapes for all times of year.

Dina's current choice was white, snowflake-shaped lights, and in the darkness I could almost imagine it was snowing. It made me miss Michigan, at least until I remembered how long those snowy months last and how dry my skin used to get from forced-air heating.

Passing Al and Karen's place, I noticed movement inside. Their car wasn't in the drive, but someone closed the curtains at the front window. Bonnie had reported Al's fall, saying he was okay but would be kept in the hospital overnight because of all his health issues. Seeing the curtains close, I figured Karen was back home, and I wanted to let her know I'd do whatever I could to help. I climbed the steps, knocked once, and then opened the door. "Karen? What did you find out?"

A hand grabbed my wrist, and a single jerk pulled me over the threshold. I let out a squeal of surprise, but before I could do more, the door slammed behind me. An arm went around my waist, and the hand that had held my wrist clamped over my mouth. All that happened so fast I didn't have time to think what to do.

"Who's that?" A young man came out of the back. Though it was dark in the trailer, I saw that he was skinny, with light hair and one of those goofy-looking beards that make a man look like a goat. In one hand he held several pill bottles. When he saw me, his voice took on a different note. "Turk, what are you—"

"She walked right in. I'm not about to let her walk out again."

"Who is she?"

"How am I supposed to know?" Turk spoke in my ear. "I'm going to take my hand away from your mouth. Answer me and we might let you live." When I nodded, he let go, and I sucked in a huge gulp of air. "Do you live here?"

"N-n-no. This is Al and Karen's place."

"Where are they?"

"Al's in the hospital. Karen's with him. I don't know when she'll be home."

"That's good, lady. You're doing good."

"Let's tie her up and go. By the time she gets loose, we'll be gone."

"She'll describe us to the cops," the one called Turk said. "I'm in the system. You're local. In two hours every lawman in the area will be looking for us."

The kid didn't like that, but he soon came up with another idea. "We have to go then. Leave the state."

"In case you never noticed," the big man said in a growling tone, "all roads out of Florida run north. They can cut us off easy."

"So we go west. We steal a boat and head for Mexico."

"And live on what? Did you happen to bring a few thousand dollars along for starter money?"

"Well, no, but—You don't mean you're going to—hurt her."

"Dickie, all that's standing between us and getting out of this is her. If she can't tell what she saw, we can walk away like we've done a dozen times already."

"But you're talking about killing a person. We can't—"

Turk spoke over my shoulder. "You got two choices, kid. My way or prison."

A twist of his body, a shrugging away of responsibility, told me he'd come down on Turk's side. "How are you going to…do it?"

"I don't know." Turk tightened his grip on my waist and put his hand back over my mouth. "It should look like an accident, so we're in the clear. Maybe she falls down the steps or drowns in the lake." He paused. "The problem is making it happen without anybody seeing us."

Rattling the bottles he held, Dickie entered into the spirit of Turk's plan. "Whoever lives here is on some heavy meds. What if the old broad took a bunch of these?"

"Good thinking. She knows the owners are gone, she decides to use their meds to kill herself."

He'd eased up on gagging me, and I spoke from behind his hand. "I would never—"

Turk cut my words off. "I'll hold her. Start feeding her pills."

I fought them, but it did no good. Even skinny Dickie outweighed me, and Turk was scary strong. If I opened my mouth to scream, Dickie dumped pills in and Turk forced my jaw closed. If I tried to spit them out, Turk smacked me on the head. Dickie picked up any pills I ejected and shoved them into my mouth again. Turk pinched my nostrils, closing off my breathing until my head spun and I swallowed. Then he'd let me get a breath, but he also whacked me again, to show that he meant business.

By the time the bottle was empty, we were all exhausted. They sat me in a chair and hunkered down on either side of me, waiting for me to lose consciousness. Tears streamed down my cheeks, and everything hurt: my arms where they'd held me, my throat from the pills, and the rest of me from struggling to get away. In only minutes I began to feel like the world was slowing, slowing, slowing. Turk put his face inches from mine and said something. It sounded like Charlie Brown's teacher talking. The last thing I remember is him smiling at me. It wasn't a friendly kind of smile.

Chapter Fifty-Four

Earl (Earl & Wilma) Saturday, 6:10 p.m.

An afternoon round of golf can get really long, especially on weekends, since the people ahead of you dictate how your play goes. We trailed several extra-slow groups that day, and only one of them let us play through. The others seemed unaware we were cooling our heels behind them. Daylight was gone by the time we left the course, and with packing up and driving back, I didn't get home until after six. A note on the table from Wilma said, "At the chapel."

When she wasn't home by six-thirty, I was a little worried, but I told myself she went to Alice's for tea or something. Still, she's almost always home by six, since we eat supper around seven. I'll admit right here and now that I don't know one end of a kitchen from the other. Last night's casserole sat in the fridge, covered with a sheet of foil Wilma had carefully washed and reused. I wondered two things: Should I get it out and start it warming, and if so, how would I do that? There's the microwave and the toaster oven and the big oven. Which one was right for the job?

In the end I left the casserole and went for a walk. The chapel was closed and dark, and I didn't meet Wilma on the street. Knowing she didn't want me checking up on her, I didn't do what I wanted to, which was start knocking on doors.

At seven-fifteen and still no Wilma, I started imagining bad things. Had she tripped in the dark and broken her leg? No, because she could call out and get help anywhere in the park. Had she been pulled into a car by some creep? Unlikely. Nobody kidnaps seventy-three-year-old women unless they're wearing diamonds. Though I tried to find un-scary reasons for Wilma's absence, it doesn't do much good to tell your mind not to worry when it's already doing it.

Still unwilling to make her mad at me, I did a visual check of her friends' places. At night, you can tell who's in a trailer—well, maybe not who exactly, but lights inside let you see outlines. At Ron and Julie's I saw two heads in front of the TV. At Tommy's across the street, Alice was doing something in the kitchen while Tommy either cleared or set the table. I went to the home of the friend who sits next to her in the choir. Bonnie and her husband sat outside with two guests, neither of them my wife, so I said hello and went on. Next was Karen and Al's. One of the guys had reported that Al was in the hospital. If he was doing okay, Karen might be home, and Wilma might have stopped to offer whatever help and comfort she could.

The place was dark, and the driveway was empty. Disappointed, I stopped to think where to try next. As I hesitated, something moved at a side window, a flash of white across the inner blackness. Wilma had been wearing a white sweater, and I thought maybe Karen had called and asked her to get something from the trailer.

But Wilma would have turned on the lights.

It shouldn't be my wife in there, but I was convinced it was. When you've been married to the same person for decades, their movements become so familiar they're instantly recognizable. Wilma had waved an arm in a gesture that indicated an emphatic, "No!"

Next thing I knew I was on the porch, peering through a glass panel in the door. It was murky inside, but I could make out two men bent over a figure in a recliner. Wilma. My brain struggled to comprehend what was happening. Had she had a fainting spell? The men hovered over her as if waiting to see if she'd be okay.

The whole thing made no sense. What were two strangers doing in Al's trailer? After a second I realized the men weren't trying to help Wilma. They were making sure she stayed in the chair.

Glancing around the dark porch, I saw Al's cane propped against the handrail, its metal handle glowing softly in the pale light. I picked it up, hefted it until the balance felt right, and walked softly back to the door. The men were still hovering. Wilma's head lolled to one side, and her eyelids fluttered. My pulse rose, and anger I haven't felt in a long time took over my whole body. I rushed in with the cane raised.

"Get away from my wife!"

Both men turned toward me, their faces pale in the darkness. The smaller one reacted first. He was under my arm and out the door faster than I'd have believed anyone could move.

That left me facing the other guy, whose reaction was the complete opposite. He straightened, and I saw the flash of white teeth. "What you going to do, old man? Fight me?"

There was no sense telling him what I was going to do, so I did it. Swinging the cane in an upward arc, I caught him on the ribs. He let out a grunt of pain, but he didn't go down. One arm lowered protectively over the injured spot, but as I attempted a second blow, he reached out and grabbed the cane with his other hand. He jerked on it, trying to pull it out of my grasp. I held on, arthritis and all. A guy that big would trounce me in no time if the only weapon in the fight was under his control. Putting my free hand on the cane, I pulled and twisted, sliding it out of his grasp.

The fact that he hadn't won that round didn't dull my opponent's confidence. Raising his arms like a big old bird of prey, he grinned again. "Is that all you've got?"

Something my niece had once told me popped into my head.

"They showed us how to do a throat punch in gym class today," she'd said casually as I filled sacks with sugar beets and she tied them off. "If a guy comes at you, you're supposed to hit him hard in the throat. Coach said you can disable an attacker pretty easy that way." At the time, her words had made me sad that a sweet young woman has to learn such tactics. Now, the information became practical.

Turning the handle of the cane toward the attacker, I jabbed it directly at his Adam's apple as hard as I could. I had little faith that it would work, but the guy made a horrible choking sound and fell to his knees, snuffling for breath. Not willing to trust my victory to a single blow, I gave him a sharp jab to the gut that doubled him over and started him gagging.

Two things had to be done, but I wasn't sure which to do first. I needed to secure the guy before he recovered and came at me again. But I also needed to call 9-1-1- for Wilma, who slumped in the chair, barely conscious. Since I had the cane and could bash the guy if he tried to get up, I decided to call for help first. Except when I tapped my pocket, I realized I'd left my phone at home.

At that moment, a light came on overhead. I turned to see Julie in the doorway. "Earl, what's going on?"

"I don't know. These two guys did something to Wilma. I hurt this one but the other got away—"

"No, he didn't. He ran into Ron and me—literally. He's down, and Ron's keeping an eye on him."

The guy on the floor managed to suck in some air, and we heard a muttered curse. Leaning over him for a second Julie said, "There should be rope in the shed. Get it while I call for help." As I started past her she put out a hand. "Leave me the cane. If this jerk gives me trouble, I'll whack him again."

Chapter Fifty-Five

Ron (Ron & Julie) Saturday 6:30 p.m.

Julie and I went out for a walk before time for *Jeopardy!* We had to bundle up a little, but the stars were out in full force. I was trying to be extra nice, since her worry for Al had started to wear off, leaving room for her irritation with Tommy and me to return. I suggested the walk, since getting outside tends to put her in a mellower mood.

My knee had been feeling good, so I left my cane at home. Later I wished I'd brought it. You never know when you're going to need to clock somebody.

As we neared Al and Karen's place, we heard a commotion and saw a man come running out the door. Stumbling down the steps, he used the newel post as a fulcrum to turn himself toward the street. In his need for speed he didn't see us in the dark, which resulted in a surprise for all. Julie managed to step aside and took only a minor jostle, but I got hit full on. Bouncing off each other, the runner and I went down in different directions. He must have cracked his head a good one on the pavement, because he stayed there, stunned. I landed on my backside on the grass, but it gave my still-tender knee an unexpected jolt.

After a second the guy groaned and let loose a few curse words. Leaning over him Julie demanded, "What were you doing in Karen's house?"

He cursed again, putting both hands at the back of his head as if to see if his brain was still on the inside of his skull.

With help from my wife, I managed to get back to my feet. Over the half-conscious intruder's dull moans, we heard grunts and dull thuds coming from Al's place. Someone was fighting in there. Not trusting my leg to carry me up the steps, I whispered to Julie, "Go see what's happening in there. Don't go in. Just look."

"What about him?"

"If he moves, I'll sit on him."

The guy seemed to have regained his ability to hear and understand, because he added new cuss words. I repeated my threat, and he went silent.

Hurrying up the steps, Julie peered in through the open door. I heard her gasp, and then she did exactly what I'd told her not to do. She disappeared inside. That made me nervous, and I strained to hear what was going on while keeping an eye on my prisoner. The noises stopped, and I heard Julie ask a question. A murmur of conversation convinced me she was in no danger. Appearing briefly in the doorway she said, "I called for police and EMTs." A short time later she came outside and told me what had happened. "Is Wilma okay?" I asked.

"I don't know. I hope the ambulance gets here soon." Pausing, she said, "I think I hear it now."

Chapter Fifty-Six

Earl (Earl & Wilma) Saturday, 6:40 p.m.

Within minutes of Julie's call, we had cop cars and emergency vehicles everywhere. The EMTs found the empty pill bottle, so they figured out what pills Wilma had been forced to take. "We'll get them out of her system," a woman who didn't look old enough to vote assured me.

"Will she be okay then?"

"It hasn't been long, so if we get her stomach pumped, she should be fine." She put a hand on my arm. "It's a good thing you got here when you did."

I can't tell you what it's like to see the person you've spent most of your life with pale and still on a gurney. It was nice of the girl to say Wilma would be okay, but that's the kind of thing those people always say. "Can I ride with her?"

"Of course. We'll let you know when we've got her ready to go, but the police would like a word with you."

The officer wanted to know what had happened, but I couldn't tell him much. I didn't know who the guys were or why Wilma had gone into Al's place. In the end, the cop wrote down my name and where I'd be, and I climbed into the ambulance with Wilma. Looking worried, Julie promised she and Ron would follow as soon as possible. Then the doors closed, and we were off.

Chapter Fifty-Seven

Ron (Ron & Julie) Saturday 7:00 p.m.

When the ambulance pulled away, the police officers interviewed Julie and me. We'd told them enough to get the two men restrained and taken into custody. EMTs didn't see either as badly injured, though the small guy whined about how much his head hurt and the larger man's raspy voice indicated his larynx was badly bruised. He managed to rasp out "Lawyer," and his companion immediately followed suit.

Julie and I told what we knew, which wasn't much. Other park residents had come outside to see what the commotion was, and they whispered to each other, their expressions grave. A month before, Julie had been attacked by a murderer. Now she was again involved in crime, though she was neither perpetrator nor victim.

"The skinny guy came barreling out of this trailer, and we knew that wasn't a good thing," Julie told the cop. "Karen's with her husband at the hospital. The guy ran right into Ron here, and when he fell, his hit his head. Ron subdued him, and I went to check the house. Inside I saw Earl brandishing a cane at a man I'd never seen before. Wilma, Earl's wife, was in a chair, unconscious. I called for help, Earl tied up the intruder. That's all we know."

"These men couldn't be friends of the owners?"

Julie gave the kid a look. "Do your friends visit when you aren't home, leave the lights off, and attack women who come to the door?"

The cop coughed. "Are you sure that's what happened?"

"What else could it be?"

He tried for a superior tone. "I try not to draw conclusions before I have all the facts, ma'am."

"Well, let me give you more facts. Wilma and Earl are the kindest, gentlest people you'll ever meet. If Earl whacked that guy with a stick, he was defending his wife. Those men had to be burgling the house."

He seemed doubtful. "What would they have been looking for?"

The answer came to me in a flash, and I said it aloud. "Drugs."

"Sir?"

"This is an over-55 park. The residents have lots of prescriptions. Trailers aren't easy to secure. The doors have chintzy locks, and too many of our people never lock up anyway. It would be easy to sneak in and steal people's drugs."

"We haven't had any reports of that."

Julie spoke up. "I have. Lately people have complained they're missing pills, not whole bottles, but they have fewer than they should. If those guys were breaking in and taking a few pills at a time, most residents wouldn't notice."

Behind me someone said, "Betty said yesterday that she got shorted on her painkillers. She called her doctor, but they said she wasn't due for more yet."

The cop was writing it down. "Betty?"

"She's over on Stork," the guy replied. "Number 12. I bet she'll let you dust the bottles for prints."

The cop's partner came out of Al's place carrying a small plastic bag with an assortment of pills inside. "This was under one of the recliners," she said. "Looks like it got dropped during the struggle."

Our guy nodded, certain now that we were correct. "They only took a few, so the person blames either his memory or the pharmacy."

"Wilma was unlucky enough to walk in while they were helping themselves to Al's prescription drugs," I said. "They couldn't let her go."

Julie shivered. "I don't know how Earl found her, but it's a good thing he did."

Chapter Fifty-Eight

Wilma (Earl & Wilma) Sunday 9:00 a.m.

I realized I was in a strange place before I opened my eyes. There were beeps and buzzes, some near my head, others farther away. I was in a hospital.

I waited a few seconds, trying to figure out what had happened. I didn't recall being in the car, so it couldn't have been a traffic accident. My doctor says I'm healthy, so I didn't think I'd had a heart attack.

Then I remembered those two men standing over me, waiting as I lost consciousness. What had happened to save me?

I opened my eyes and found Julie sitting in a chair by my bed. "Hey, girlie. It's good to see you awake."

I had to try twice before getting my question out. "E—Earl?"

"I sent him to get some breakfast. He's been a mess all night long, wanting you to wake up but also wanting you to rest and get those drugs out of your system."

"They m-made me swallow pills."

"That's what we figured. You're okay now, though your stomach is probably sore. They had to pump it."

"Yes." After a few seconds I said, "How come I'm not dead?"

"Earl." Julie smiled. "You should have seen him, Wilma. He scared one of those creeps so bad he ran away. Then he took on the big one." She shook her head. "Old farmers must be tough, because your Earl managed to put that muscle-bound goon on the floor."

"Earl beat up Turk?"

"If that's his name. When he saw what they'd done to you, Earl went a little Rambo."

Earl came in right then. His face lit when he saw that I was awake, and I put out a hand. Taking it, he leaned close. "Are you feeling okay, Sweetheart?"

Julie waved and backed out of the room, leaving us in private. "Julie says you saved my life."

He looked down, embarrassed, but his voice held a note of pride. "I wasn't about to let two hooligans hurt my best girl."

"How did you find me?"

"When you didn't come back, I went looking. I know you don't like it when I worry, but it felt like something wasn't right."

"Earl Schmidt," I said, "you are one amazing man. I've always loved you, and now—well, now I'm willing to admit that I need you too. You're always watching out for me, and that's a good thing."

"We watch out for each other, Honey. I'd starve to death without you. My half of our partnership is keeping us as safe as I can."

"Well, you scored a big fat ten this time."

That was all we said on the topic, but I had learned two things. First, Earl's fussing is all for the very good reason that he loves me. He's better than I am at looking ahead and predicting what bad things might happen. And he's better at physical stuff. I don't know what I'd have done if our roles were reversed, so I'm glad it was him that had to rescue me and not vice versa.

The other thing I realized is that being irritated with your mate doesn't mean you don't love him anymore. Irritation is temporary, the result of bumping against each other for years and years. Give it a while and love overcomes irritation, any day of the week.

Chapter Fifty-Nine

Tommy (Tommy & Alice) Sunday, 10:00 a.m.

It didn't take long for rumors to spread about what had happened, but I heard the story direct from Ron the next morning. We were discussing it over coffee when Detective O'Connor arrived, so Ron went inside and got him a cup too. Julie came outside with him, pulling on a jacket, since it was only 60 degrees. It was nice in the sunlight, though, and warming fast.

"The guy your buddy Earl took out is Theodore Cabot, also known as Turk," O'Connor told us. "He's spent time in prison for burglary and dealing drugs. The other guy is Dickie Blake, who often cuts through the park to reach a fishing spot he likes on the far side of Pelican Lake. As he passed through, Dickie realized how easy it would be to steal stuff. People don't lock their cars, and they leave belongings outside.

"He started by taking a bike. When he got away with that, Dickie helped himself to a few more things that had been left outdoors. After a few weeks, he started breaking into places that looked empty. In one he found some pill bottles someone had left behind, so he helped himself to a few." O'Connor's lip curled. "Dickie's willing to try anything that's likely to get him high. Eventually he started going in when residents weren't at home, seeing what they had for prescription drugs."

"People noticed," I told him. "There were reports of a peeper, but they didn't sound believable, since the descriptions varied."

"Oh, my gosh, Ron." Julie grabbed his arm. "Remember that

night we thought someone had been in our house?"

"I had some Vicodin left over from my surgery," he said. "I should count to see if any are missing."

"How would you know?" I asked.

Julie gave him a playful slap. "Because he's Mr. Tough Guy. They gave him ten, and he took two, maybe three."

"Two," Ron informed us. "No sense getting hooked on that stuff."

"Will you look, please?" O'Connor asked, and Ron went inside.

When he came out, his expression was grave. "Three left."

"Someone took five pills."

"He could get maybe fifty bucks for those on the street. Not a bad profit for zero investment. All it takes is guts."

Julie looked horrified. Ron looked sick. It's always a shock to learn your home has been entered by a stranger with evil intentions.

Which led me to think of Xanax, which Alice has for anxiety. She has a scrip, but she's been trying to wean herself off them, so the pills sit in the medicine cabinet. I went over to our house and checked. The bottle said there were 30 tablets. I counted ten left.

"Alice, have you been taking your Xanax?"

Her first response was anger. "Is it any of your business—"

Stepping toward her, I took her in my arms, which I've found is a good way to calm her down. "Honey, those men the police arrested last night have been stealing drugs from resident's homes. O'Connor needs to know if you're missing pills."

"Oh. Sorry, Tommy, I—"

"It's okay."

She estimated she was missing at least ten pills. We went outside together to tell the others.

O'Connor whistled softly. "You know, it isn't a bad scheme. As long as they aren't greedy, they get away with it. Not bad for an ex-con and a former juvenile delinquent."

"How did the bigger guy—Turk—get involved?"

"They're cousins. Dickie bragged to Turk about how easy it was to score drugs here. Turk wanted in, but for profit, not for personal use. What Turk wants, he apparently gets."

"I doubt he'll get what he wants from the state of Florida," Ron commented.

O'Connor started to rise, but Ron and I met each other's gaze in silent decision. "Don't go yet," I told him. "We've got the Nashville thing figured out, and it's time we share what we know."

Chapter Sixty

Ron (Ron & Julie) Wednesday, 9:30 a.m.

Detective O'Connor showed up at my door two days after we told him the truth about our investigation. Julie was at the clubhouse, doing last-minute stuff for the unveiling party for The Project, but I invited him to sit, poured him an iced tea, and offered cookies. After years with Julie, I'm not completely uncivilized.

"Because of what you told us, the police up in Nashville looked again at hairs found on the woman who was murdered. Apparently she pulled them out as she struggled with the killer. There was no DNA testing back then, but the hairs were preserved, along with the other evidence. Turns out they came from a man named James Dunlop, who owned the apartment house where it happened."

"You said the original detective called the landlord odd."

O'Connor nodded. "If your guy hadn't looked so guilty, the cops might have looked closer at Dunlop. He was arrested a few years later for assaulting a woman, so his DNA was on file. He went to prison, where he got into a fight with another inmate and died of his injuries."

"Poetic justice." I turned to my main concern. "What's going to happen to Hank?"

"Nashville's done with him. It's up to the United States Army now." O'Connor raised a brow. "I understand you got him a lawyer. What's his opinion?"

"He'll get a dishonorable discharge for sure, but the attorney doubts they'll do more than that. It happened fifty years ago. Hank's old and has a sick wife. They'll ask for clemency, appealing to the army tribunal, Hank's congressman, and even his senator."

"Covering all the bases. Sounds like a lawyer to me." O'Connor stood, taking one more of Julie's chocolate chip cookies for the road. "Again, thanks for the work you did. We look good to the Nashville guys, and I look good to my superiors."

"Anytime, Detective." I followed him outside. Alice was leaving her place, and she waved before heading toward the clubhouse, on her way to help Julie get things ready.

"How did Mrs. Murgasson's visit with her nephew go?" he asked.

I frowned. "They haven't had any visitors. And I've never heard her speak of a nephew."

O'Connor stopped for a moment, his head tilted a little like a robot fed information that doesn't compute. Then he let out a little huff of air. "I see."

"I'm heading to the clubhouse for the official unveiling of Julie's poster project," I told him. "Want to come along?"

"Duty calls." O'Connor smiled. "But I'm going to stop at the office and see Marlene, so I can give you a ride down there if you like. Save wear and tear on that new knee."

When O'Connor dropped me off, there was a steady stream of people entering the hall. Joining the line, I found myself directly behind Matthew and Taffy Nowicki. Taffy was talking to someone ahead of her in line, and Matthew turned to me.

"Pretty exciting, huh? Your wife did a lot of work for this."

"Yes, she's been busy. It took a lot of organization."

Matthew smirked. "It wasn't all that well organized. I got asked three different times where I was on the date she picked."

"Hmm." That's about all you can say when Matthew starts in.

His expression turned sly. "I gave her an answer that suits her little project, but I'll tell you where I really was on that date if you want."

That wasn't an easy one. I was kind of interested in where Matthew might have gone that he hadn't told anyone about, even Taffy, but I also can't stand the guy, so I hate to encourage him.

It didn't matter; he was going to tell me anyway. "That summer, I spent a week in the mountains with a patriotic group called the Fusiliers. We learned how the government lies to us all the time and how we have to be ready to rise up when the time comes."

Apparently 'the time' hadn't come in the last fifty-three years, but I suppose readiness is good. "You trained for that?"

"Well, sorta. I didn't stay for the whole thing."

"Why not?"

"All the noise made me nervous," he said. "I started getting bad headaches, and it made me sick to my stomach. The leader said it was probably best if I went back to Middletown and rested up."

And so ended the budding career of the next Che Guevara.

Earl and Wilma had arrived ahead of me, but they waited inside until I caught up. Taking leave of Matthew, I joined them as Tommy waved us over to a table.

"My job was to get us seats up front." Tommy waved his phone. "And to take pictures for Karen and Al."

"Is he feeling better?"

Tommy grinned. "He says people shouldn't get all bent out of shape about a little fall."

At that point Nan took the stage, followed by a slightly reluctant Julie. I knew she was nervous about the amount of hoopla that had attached itself to her project. "It's bits of paper," she'd moaned that morning at breakfast. "The display can't dance or sing or do tricks, so why does everyone have to come in a big bunch to look at them?"

"You know enough about senior communities by now," I told her. "Any excuse for a party."

The atmosphere was definitely party-like, and Nan was in her element. "You all know Julie Rogers had this fun idea that she'd pick a date and ask everyone in the park where they were living at that time." Nan put a hand on her chest. "Now, I helped a teensy bit, and I have to tell you it's really cool to see where we were back then. And aren't you glad that we all ended up here, friends and neighbors in the nicest park in Florida?"

There were cheers at that, and Nan waited until they died down. "Okay. Let's unveil the posters."

Julie removed a light blue swath of fabric from the right-hand side of the display. That was Europe and Africa, and there were several pushpins there with thread stretching to labels that named the people who'd been there in 1967. Some were in England and Scotland, some on the European mainland, and one lonely pushpin was in central Africa. The crowd clapped, and Julie gave them a nervous smile of appreciation.

Next she went to the left side and removed a second length of fabric. Behind it were Asia, Australia, and South America. There were only two pushpins in South America, one in Columbia and one way down south in Argentina. Australia had two, and a couple I knew to be from Brisbane cheered and whooped to celebrate their representation.

Finally Julie removed the center drape, revealing the United States, Canada, and Mexico. The latter had only a few pins, but the two northern nations bristled with bright colors, concentrated on the eastern half of the map but represented everywhere. Labels above and below had strings going every which way. It was an impressive sight, and I was proud of what she'd done. Applause showed the crowd's appreciation for her work, and Julie's face turned as pink as the tropical shirt she wore.

Holding up a finger, Julie signaled more to come. Stepping off stage, she came back with two sheets of poster board taped together. On them, she had listed the people who helped with the project. In large letters were WILMA SCHMIDT, ALICE MURGASSON, and KAREN DOBSON. Under that in slightly smaller letters were the names of all the volunteers, starting with JESSICA LATRAN and ending with NAN SHAW. Atop the poster board she'd cut out the letters T-H-A-N-K-S and glued stars and glitter to them. The audience cheered again, and the people named blushed and smiled at being recognized.

Nan waited until things settled down before speaking again. "I know we all appreciate Julie's hard work on this. Once the program is done, you're welcome to come up and get a closer look. We plan to leave the display up until spring, so even our late arrivals will get a chance to see it."

More applause, and then Nan went on. "Now we've asked several people to give a brief account of what they were doing on our chosen date…if you can all remember back that far." Everyone laughed, but in all likelihood, there were people there who remembered 1967 better than they recalled breakfast this morning. "We picked an artist, a soldier, a Peace Corps volunteer, and a poet. We figured that covers the '60s pretty well."

More applause, and then Nan said, "When they're finished, the council has bought ice cream and toppings, so each person to make their own sundae."

That brought the most applause yet. Julie caught my eye, and I knew what she was thinking. Anyone unimpressed with the posters would at least get ice cream. That's life in a retiree community: We look for entertainment, we look for connections, and more often than not, we look for food.

Notes

Dear Reader:

If you enjoyed this book, please consider placing a review somewhere others will see it. Authors rely on word of mouth to spread the news of a new book or series, and no one does that better than happy readers!

Thank you for supporting what we writers love to do!

Maggie

Visit Maggie online at https://maggiepill.maggiepillmysteries.com

The Sleuth Sisters Mysteries (cozy Michigan)

If you like lighter mysteries, and if you have sisters, had sisters, or know a little about sisters, you'll love this series.

The Sleuth Sisters
3 Sleuths, 2 Dogs, 1 Murder
Murder in the Boonies
Sleuthing at Sweet Springs

Eat, Drink, & Be Wary
Peril, Plots, and Puppies
Captured, Escape, Repeat

Trailer Park Tales

Once Upon a Trailer Park (Book #1)

Books by Peg Herring

The Simon & Elizabeth Mysteries (Tudor Era Historical)

Her Highness' First Murder
Poison, Your Grace
The Lady Flirts with Death
Her Majesty's Mischief

***

The Loser Mysteries (Contemporary Mystery/Suspense)

Killing Silence
Killing Memories
Killing Despair

***

Clan Macbeth Historical Romance (medieval Scotland)

Macbeth's Niece
Double Toil & Trouble

***

The Kidnap Capers

KIDNAP.org
Pharma Con

The Trouble with Dad

***

Standalone Mysteries

Somebody Doesn't Like Sarah Leigh (contemporary cozy mystery)
Her Ex-GI P.I. ('60s-era traditional mystery)
Not Dead Yet... ('60s-era paranormal mystery)
Shakespeare's Blood (thriller)

Visit Maggie's alter ego online at https://pegherring.com

www.ingramcontent.com/pod-product-compliance
Ingram Content Group UK Ltd.
Pitfield, Milton Keynes, MK11 3LW, UK
UKHW020132250726
13967UKWH00002B/604